DETROIT STUDIES IN MUSIC BIBLIOGRAPHY

General Editor   Bruno Nettl   University of Illinois at Urbana-Champaign

THEMATIC CATALOG OF THE WORKS OF JEREMIAH CLARKE

Thomas F. Taylor

Detroit Studies in Music Bibliography Number Thirty Five

Information Coordinators 1977 Detroit

Copyright 1977 by Thomas F. Taylor
Library of Congress Catalog Card Number 75-23551   International Standard Book Number 911772-84-7
Book design by Vincent Kibildis   Printed and bound in the United States of America
Published by Information Coordinators, Inc., 1435-37 Randolph Street, Detroit, Michigan 48226

On the cover and pages two and three:
Fish Street Hill, London, at the close of the seventeenth century. The Monument, designed by
Sir Christopher Wren and built in 1671-1677, marks the place where The Great Fire of 1666 broke out.

CONTENTS

PREFACE

ONE OF THE FIRST STEPS NECESSARY to the study of the complete works of a composer is the compilation of a thematic catalog of his works. The most complete catalog of the music of Jeremiah Clarke (*ca.* 1673-1707) available to date is a twenty-seven page appendix to the author's dissertation (PhD, Music History, Northwestern University, 1967). This is a list with no themes, based on such sources as the Hughes *Catalogue of Manuscript Music in the British Museum,* the Snapper *British Union Catalogue of Early Music Printed Before the Year 1801,* and the partial lists in *Die Musik in Geschichte und Gegenwart* and *Grove's Dictionary of Music and Musicians.* A number of the works were looked at by means of microfilms and photographs, but none of the original sources themselves were inspected; nor were libraries searched for possible sources not included in the above lists.

This type of search and inspection was necessary for the completion and publication of a comprehensive annotated thematic catalog. The search was carried on during May-August 1970, aided by generous grants from the University of Michigan Rackham School and the Penrose Fund of the American Philosophical Society. The holdings of the appropriate libraries were consulted and a large number of changes and additions were made to the information collected before that time.

It is difficult to single out individuals from among the many who were significantly helpful in the various stages of work on this catalog. Without the financial assistance from the Rackham School, and the Penrose Fund of the American Philosophical Society mentioned above, the work would still be a dream. In the initial stage of my interest in the works of Jeremiah Clarke, John F. Ohl gave of his time in sharing his understanding of the Baroque as he guided work on the dissertation.

As work commenced on the present catalog, Edward Soenlein was of great assistance in setting up the project. As the author worked in England, he was indebted to Charles Cudworth, whose previous work on Clarke was always sound and who provided duplication and other assistance at the Pendlebury Music Library. Another dissertation on the works of Clarke was in progress at Cambridge, and its author, Christopher Powell, was in residence at nearby Emmanuel College. Mr. Powell was most generous in sharing his materials and ideas about our mutual subject.

The librarians and staff at the following libraries provided assistance and materials as they were needed. In Great Britain:

> Public Library, Birmingham
> Public Library, Cardiff
> Fitzwilliam Museum, Cambridge
> St. John's College, Cambridge
> Rowe Library, King's College, Cambridge
> Carlisle Cathedral, Carlisle
> Cathedral Library, Durham
> University Library, Edinburgh
> Cathedral Library, Ely

Cathedral Library, Hereford
Cathedral Library, Lichfield
Royal Academy of Music, London
British Museum, London
Royal College of Music, London
Guildhall Library, London
St. Paul's Cathedral, London
Public Libraries, Manchester
Chetham's Library, Manchester
Bodleian Library, Oxford
Christ Church Library, Oxford
Magdalen College, Oxford
St. Michael's College, Tenbury Wells
Cathedral Library, Worcester
Minster Library, York

In the United States:

Huntington Library, San Marino, California
Newberry Library, Chicago
Northwestern University Library, Evanston
Library of Congress, Washington, D.C.
University of Michigan Libraries, Ann Arbor
University of Texas Libraries, Austin

Upon returning from England, the writer was aided by Ms. Cina Stevens who sorted information and typed. In the final stages of completing the catalog, thanks should go to the University of Michigan Rackham School for extending the grant to supply further editorial and clerical assistance from Ms. Priscilla Weaver. As the work was reviewed for publication, Mr. Nicolas Temperley of the University of Illinois generously supplied suggestions and a number of additional printed sources for the Anthems. These have been incorporated. Thanks also are due to Ms. Elaine Gorzelski and Mr. Vincent Kibildis of Information Coordinators whose composition layout and design of the book resulted in greater clarity for the reader. Finally, thanks are due to my wife, Nancy, who lived through all the stages with patience and understanding, lending a critical eye when it was needed.

ABBREVIATIONS AND LIBRARY SIGLA

Performing Sources	rec	recorder (often called flute)
	ob	oboe
	tpt	trumpet
	timp	timpani
	str	strings (four-part unless otherwise noted)
	vln	violin
	vla	viola
	'cello	violoncello
	Bc (bc)	basso continuo
	satb	soprano, alto, tenor, bass soloists
	SATB	soprano, alto, tenor, bass chorus
Other Abbreviations	ed.	edition (*pl.* eds.)
	fol.	folio (*pl.* fols.)
	inc	incomplete
	MS	manuscript (*pl.* MSS)
	no.	number (*pl.* nos.)
	obl.	obbligato
	p.	page (*pl.* pp.)
	rit	ritornello
	s.sh.fol.	single sheet folio format of publication
	v (rev)	verso (folio 47v is the reverse side of folio 47)
	vol.	volume (*pl.* vols.)
Library Sigla		**EIRE / Ireland**
	Dcc	Christ Church Cathedral, Dublin
	Dpc	St. Patrick's Cathedral, Dublin
	Dtc	Trinity College, Dublin
		Great Britain
	AY	Bucks County Record Office, Aylesbury
	Bp	Public Library, Birmingham
	Bu	University Library, Birmingham
	CA	Cathedral Libraries, Canterbury
	CDp	Public Library, Cardiff

Abbreviations and Library Sigla

Library Sigla

Great Britain

Cfm	Fitzwilliam Museum, Cambridge
Cjc	St. John's College, Cambridge
Ckc	King's College, Cambridge
Cmc	Magdalene College, Cambridge
Ctc	Trinity College, Cambridge
CL	Carlisle Cathedral, Carlisle
DRc	Cathedral Library, Durham
EL	Cathedral Library, Ely
En	National Library of Scotland, Edinburgh
Eu	University Library, Edinburgh
EX	University Library, Exeter
Ge	Euing Music Library, Glasgow
GL	Cathedral Library, Gloucester
H	Cathedral Library, Hereford
Lam	Royal Academy of Music, London
Lbm	British Museum, London
Lcm	Royal College of Music, London
LF	Cathedral Library, Lichfield
Lg	Gresham College, Guildhall Library, London
LI	Cathedral Library, Lincoln
Lsp	St. Paul's Cathedral, London
Mc	Chetham's Library, Manchester
Mp	Public Libraries, Manchester
NH	Record Office, Northampton
Ob	Bodleian Library, Oxford
Och	Christ Church, Oxford
Omc	Magdalen College, Oxford
PB	Cathedral Library, Peterborough
T	St. Michael's College, Tenbury
WB	Minster Library, Wimborne
WRec	Eton College, Windsor
WO	Cathedral Library, Worcester
Y	Minster Library, York

United States

AUS	University of Texas Library, Austin
Cn	Newberry Library, Chicago
Eu	Northwestern University Library, Evanston
SM	Huntington Library, San Marino
Wc	Library of Congress, Washington, D.C.
WS	Folger Shakespeare Library, Washington, D.C.

Introduction and Guide to the Catalog

Since few of Clarke's works have been dated with accuracy, this catalog lists the works by category and in alphabetical order within each subcategory. The first two digits indicate the genre and the specific type of that particular work. The last digit gives the number of the piece in the alphabetical listing of all works in that type. For example, the "Prince of Denmark's March" is number 435. The first digit is four since the piece is an instrumental composition. The second digit is three or four since the work is a trumpet tune. The work is number six in an alphabetical listing of trumpet tunes, which list begins with number 430; hence the piece is number 435. The total scheme of the numbering system is listed in the Contents. Please note that the total scheme allows for future entries.

Each entry includes the following information:

1. Thematic catalog number.
2. Title (alternate titles in parentheses).
3. Sources of text, if known (Bible verses, authors, etc.).
4. Performing forces, using the abbreviations found on page 9.
5. One-line musical incipit of each work or major section. In a few cases, the incipits are in a two-line score in order to illustrate more of the texture.
6. Manuscript numbers. Each manuscript containing works by Clarke is numbered and listed in the Index on page 103.
7. Printed collections from before 1800. All collections are listed in the Index on page 121. Reference to each collection is made by a special siglum, such as COL 1 for *A Collection of Approved Anthems*.

If a source, manuscript or printed, seems particularly preferable for reference because it predates the others, or because it is more accurate than other sources, it appears in italics in the main body of the catalog. This is not to say that the other sources are without value.

8. Remarks on the sources, literature on the work, etc.

Jeremy Clark musick master

CHURCH MUSIC

Anthems

Behold God is my salvation. See No. **500**.

100 Blessed is he that considereth. Psalm 41:1-3. tb/SATB

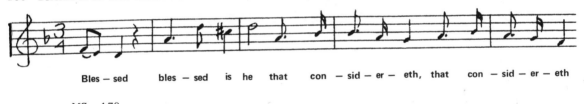

Bles — sed   bles — sed   is   he   that   con — sid — er — eth,   that   con — sid — er — eth

MS   178

101 Bow down thine ear, O Lord. Psalm 86:1, 3, 4, 5, 9, 10, 19. Organ (Bc/obl.)   atb/SATB

Bow   down thine   ear   O   Lord   and   hear   me

MSS   64, 83, 96, 176, *194*, 195, 208-212, 214-217, 233, 241-243, 299, *313*, 314, 316-319, 321, 331, 335, 341, 343-347, 356, 359, 361
Printed collection   HAR 7

Hear my crying, O God. See No. **501**.

He shall send down from on high. See remarks under No. **105**.

How long shall I seek counsel. See remarks under No. **102**.

LEFT:
Jeremy Clark Musick Master.
Drawing in black lead by George Vertue (1684-1756).
From the Collection of Edward Croft-Murray, Richmond (Surrey).
Used by permission.

102   How long wilt thou forget me?   Psalm 13:1-6.   Bc.   a/SATB

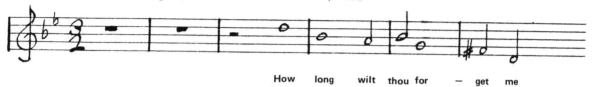

How   long   wilt   thou for   —   get   me

MSS   14, 20, 32, 64, 69, 77-79, 82, 86, 89, 90, 93, 95, 98, 100, 105, 110, 112-115, 118-120, 122, 125, 126, 129, 130, 132-136, 148, 149, *151*, 164, 192, 195, 208-210, 218, 222-224, 226, 227, 229, 231, 233, 240-243, 245, 255, 256, 263, 268, 269, 277, 288 (inc), 290, 291 (inc), 292, 296-297, 299, 309, *313*, 316-319, 321, 328, 333, 335, 337, 341, 343-347, 352

Printed collections   CAT 5 / DIV 5, 6, 7, 8, 11 / ROY 1 (inc) / SAC 4

Remarks   An organ accompaniment of the final chorus and a short account of the composer are in *MS 164* (Lbm Add. 31120) in the hand of Vincent Novello from about 1831 (see No. **561**).   The final chorus appears as a full anthem, "I will sing of the Lord" (see ROY 1 and *MS 164*).   A figured bass for organ (*MS 32*) is erroneously listed in the Cfm catalog as being a fragment of an anthem, "How long shall I seek counsel."   Those words are actually the organist's cue to the second section of this anthem.

I am the resurrection.   See No. **502**.

103   I will exalt Thee.   Bc.   atb/SATB

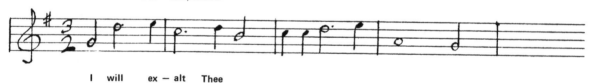

I   will   ex — alt   Thee

MS   289 (organ part only)

104   I will give thanks.   Organ (obl.)   a/SATB

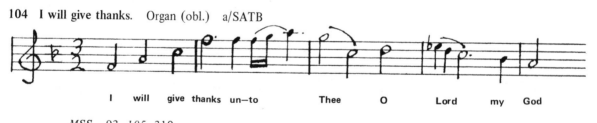

I   will   give thanks un—to   Thee   O   Lord   my   God

MSS   93, *105*, 310

105   I will love Thee, O Lord my strength.   Psalm 18:1-7, 13, 16, 21.   Organ.   tb/SATB

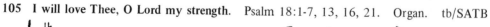

I   will   love   Thee   O   Lord   my   strength

MSS   3, 4, 6, 9, 13, 15, 18, 19, 21, 29, 36-42, 44, 51, 52, 55-59, 62, 63, 65, 67, 69, 73-75, 81-84, 87, 93, 96-97, 103, 105-107, 109-111, 113-121, 123-128, 130, 137-139, 144, 145, 147, 148, 152, 153, *161*, 182, 192, *194*, 195, 207-210, 212-219, 221, 225, 231, 233-235, 237, 239-243, 248, 255, 268, 271, 277, 286 (inc), 292-297, 299, 312, *313*, 316-320, 323, 328, 330, 332, 333, 335-338, 340, 348-349, 352, 354, 356, 359-361, 363

Printed collections   CAT 4, 5 / HAR 5, 6 / SAC 1 / SIX 1

Remarks An organ part for this anthem by Vincent Novello is in Lcm VI.A.6. (8), pp. 1010-1017. The final chorus appears as a full anthem, "He shall send down from on high" in Christopher Dearnly's *The Treasury of English Church Music,* Vol. 3, pp. 122-123.

106 **I will love Thee, O Lord** (Thanksgiving anthem). Psalm 18:1, 2, 32, 38, 41, 39, 46. Organ. atb/SATB

I will love Thee I will love Thee O – – – – Lord my strength

MSS 1, 10, 12, 26 (inc), 34, 176, *195*, 264, 283, 299, 301, *313*, 316-319, 343-344, 346-347, 363
Remarks This anthem is entirely different from No. **105** except for the first two lines of text. The two are understandably often confused with each other in cataloging. No. **106** was composed for performance at St. Paul's on August 23, 1705 to celebrate Marlborough's victory against the French by forcing the lines of Brabant at Elixem.

107 **I will magnify Thee.** Psalm 30:1-4, 11, 12b. Organ (obl.) saatb/SSATTB

I will mag – ni – fy Thee O – Lord

MSS 29, *108a*, 310
Remarks A different anthem with the same opening text by Tho. Clarke is on pages 142-144 of *The Divine Companion,* 3rd edition, 1709.

I will sing of the Lord. See remarks under No. **102.**

I will sing unto the Lord. See remarks under No. **115.**

108 **My song shall be of mercy.** Organ. TTB

My song shall be of mer – cy and judgment

Printed collections DIV *1, 2, 3, 4* / HAR 2 / RUD 1 / SAC 2

109 **O be joyful in God, all ye lands.** Psalm 66. Organ. a/SATB

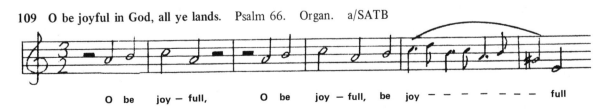

O be joy – full, O be joy – full, be joy – – – – – – – full

MSS 69, 139, *151*, 176, 201, 292, 331, 339
Printed collection DIV *11*
Remarks Composed for the annual meeting of the Sons of the Clergy, 26 November, 1706.

O Jerusalem thou that killest. See No. **503**.

110 O Lord God of my salvation. Psalm 88. Organ. satb, attb/SAATBB

O Lord God of my sal — va — tion

MSS 5, 8, 11, 12, 19-21, 47, 71, 74-77, 79-82, 84-86, 88, 90, 93-95, 97, 98, 100, 120, 123, 125-128, 130, 131, 138, 140-142, 146, 164, 187, 192, 202, 206, 218, 222-228, 238, 239, 245, 248, 249, 255, 258, 270-271, 273, 275-277, 287, 299, 300, 303, 334, 342-347, 349

Printed collections CAT 4 / COL 1 / HAR 7 / ROY 1 / SET 1 / TEN 1

Remarks An organ accompaniment to this anthem and a short account of the composer are in *MS 164* (Lbm Add. 31120) in Vincent Novello's hand from about 1831. In ROY 1, the work is attributed to Purcell. Zimmerman incorrectly attributes it to Richardson (Purcell, p. 432).

111 O Lord, rebuke me not. Psalm 6. Organ. t/SATB

O Lord re — buke me not in thine in — dig — na — tion

MSS 299, 301, *313*, 330

Remarks Listed in Myles B. Foster, *Anthems . . .* as being in Lsp. Copy not located.

112 O Lord we gat not. Psalm 44:3, 4, 6-9. Organ. atb/SATB

MSS 305-308, *316-319*, 321

113 Praise the Lord, O Jerusalem. Psalm 147:12; Isaiah 49:23; Psalm 47:8; Psalm 21:13. Organ. SATB

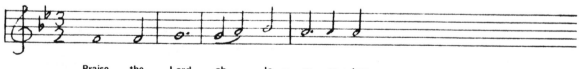

Praise the Lord, oh Je — ru — sa — lem

MSS 7, 20, 21, 27, 29, 33, 34, 36, 37, 39-47, 53-59, 63-65, 68, 71, 72, 74-78, 81-84, 87, 93, 96-97, 103-104, 109, 110, 113-115, 118-120, 122, 124-125, 128, 130, 132, 138, 142, 143, 147, 148, *162*, 188, 192, *194*, 195, 196, 197, 203, 206, 209-219, 228, 230, 232, 236, 238, 241-243, 248, 249, 255, 262, 288, 292-295, 297-298, 302, 312, 314, 317, 319, 320, 325, 329, 335, 353, 357-358, 362, 363

Printed collections BRO 2 / CAT 5 / CHO 4, 6, 7 / COL 3 / COM 3, 4 / DIV 10 / EXC 1 / HAR 2 / PSA 4

114 Praise the Lord, O my soul. Psalm 103:1-3. SAB

Praise   the   Lord   O   my   soul,   and   all that   is   with — in   me   praise

MS   102

Printed collections   BOO 1, 2, 3, 4 / BRO 1 / CHO 3, 5 / COL 2 / COM 2 / DIV *1*, 2, 3, 4, 12 / INT 1 / PSA 3, 5 / ROY 2, 3 / SAC 2 (rhythm altered)

Remarks   The work "appears in a large number of parochial collections in gradually altered forms, usually without attribution to Clarke; evidently it was transmitted orally across the country" (Nicolas Temperley in a letter to the author, 1974).   One short anthem with the same text as the present one appears in W. Tans'ur's *The Royal Harmony* . . . London, 1755, p. 177; 1760, p. 210; 1764-1765, p. 208, with the statement "originally set by Mr. Jeremy Clark, Medius by W. Tans'ur."   This piece does not appear to resemble No. **114**, but as Mr. Temperley suggests, is possibly derived from it at several removes.   No. **114** may be found in a 1965 edition by Mason Martens, published by the Concordia Publishing House.

115 Praise the Lord, O my soul. Psalm 103:1; Psalm 104:1, 2, 5, 24, 14, 13, 10, 32, 33. Organ (obl.) atb/SATB

Praise   the   Lord   O —   — my   soul

MSS   1, 26 (inc), 45, 83, 96, *264*, *313*, 314, 316-320, 322, 325, 363
Printed collection   CAT 4

Remarks   The organ parts for two sections may be found in *MS 26* (Cfm Mus. Ms. 152), erroneously listed in Cfm as a separate anthem, "I will sing unto the Lord."

Tell ye the daughter of Jerusalem.   See No. **505**.

116 The earth is the Lord's. Psalm 24:1-3. Bc. b(at)/SATB

The   earth   is   the   Lord's   and   all   — — —   that   therein   is

MSS   91, 92, 96, 97, 99, *194*, 233

The earth shall tremble.   A verse section of No. **115**.

117 The Lord is full of compassion. Organ. atb/SATB

The   Lord   is   full   of   com — pas — sion   and   mer — cy

MSS 2, 4, 8, 19, 21, 28, 29, 33, 36-38, 40-43, 61, 63-64, 66, 70, 74-75, 77, 78, 81-83, 86-87, 90, 93, 96, 108, 121, 123-125, 128, 130-131, 138, *151, 162*, 176, 195, 199, 201, 208-210, 212-221, 231, 239, 241-243, 246-247, 250-254, 256-257, 263, 272, 274, 291, 299, 310, *313*, 316-319, 321, 351, 356, 359-360
Printed collections CAT 4 / CHO 2 / DIV 9, *11* / HAR 2 / ROY 1

118 The Lord is king (The Union anthem). Psalm 97:1; Psalm 89:13. Organ. atb/SATB

MSS 259, *316-319*, 321

119 The Lord is my strength and my song. Organ. atb/SATB

MSS 26 (inc), 33, 35, *195*, 201, 283, 299, 311, *313*, 316-319, 321, 331
Printed collections HAR 7 / SIX 1
Remarks This work was composed as a Thanksgiving anthem, and was sung at St. Paul's on 27 June, 1706 to celebrate the victory at Ramelies.

120 This is the day. Psalm 118:24-29. Bc. atb/SATB

MSS 208-210, 212-219, *241-243*, 304, 306-308, *316-319, 321*

Thou, O God art praised in Sion. See No. **506.**

121-139 Reserved for future entries.

Sacred Songs

140 All praise to Thee. Text by Bishop Ken. Bc. s (or t)/SSB

MSS 102 (inc), 350
Printed collections DIV 13 / HAR *3*, 5, 6

141 Blest be those sweet regions. Bc. s

Blest be those sweet re — gions where e — ter — nal peace

MS 350
Printed collections HAR 4, 5, 6

142 Dorinda, weep no more. Bc. sb

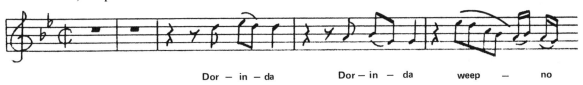

Dor — in — da   Dor — in — da   weep — no

MSS 176, *299, 313*
Remarks *MS 299* (T 310) contains only thirty-nine measures of the work. *MS 313* (T 1031) contains sixty measures.

143-149 Reserved for future entries.

Services

150 Sanctus and Gloria. Bc. atb/SATB

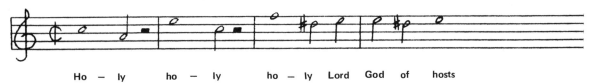

Ho — ly ho — ly ho — ly Lord God of hosts

MSS 28, 51, 244, 256, 257
Printed collection CAT 6

151 Service in C. Organ. at/SATB

We acknow — ledge thee to be the Lord

MS   313

Remarks   The above source was used by Rimbault in his *Cathedral Services,* 1847. A work called "Te deum and jubilate in c minor" is mentioned by H. W. Shaw in *Grove's Dictionary* as being in St. Paul's Cathedral Organ Book. The book was reported missing in 1966. A note attached in the front of *MS 313* (T 1031) states that the volume belonged to the Reverend Charles Badham, a minor canon of St. Paul's at the beginning of the eighteenth century. Perhaps this is the missing book.

152   Service in gamut.   Organ.   atb/SATB

MS   313

Remarks   The same comments made for No. **151** apply here. Shaw mentions a "Te deum and jubilate in G" (*Grove's*).

153   Chant in D (Psalm tone).   Organ

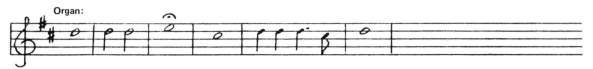

MS   46

Remarks   The above MS contains a collection of short psalm-tones by Clarke and his contemporaries. This is number 24 on folio 137.

154-159   Reserved for future entries.

Psalms and Hymns

Angel's Hymn.   See No. **520.**

160   Awake my soul awake my eyes.   Bc.   sab (t)

MSS   49, 101, 102, *156*
Printed collections   DIV *1,* 2, 3, 4

Remarks   The index in the rear of *MS 156* (Lbm Add. 22099) ascribes the work to Croft. However, in the same MS, the name, "Clark" appears after the composition in the place consistently used for the composer's name throughout the MS. Thus, the statement in the Lbm MS catalog that the "Clark" mentioned here is the copyist seems unlikely. The printed editions fix the ascription to Clarke. *MS 101* (Ckc Ms. 268) has an added tenor part. *MS 49* (DRc Ms. Mus. M. 90) uses an alternate text which begins: "Sweet is the work."

Birmingham.   See No. **169**, St. Magnus.

Bishopthorpe.   See No. **171**, St. Paul's.

Blest he whose heart with pity glows.   See No. **521**.

Brockham.   See No. **166**.

161   **Bromley.**

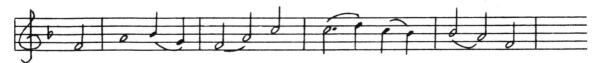

Printed collection   *The Hymnal 1940,* Nos. 163, 171, second tunes
Remarks   No earlier sources were found. However, melodic similarities to Kingston (No. **165**) and St. Magnus (No. **169**) suggest it to be by Clarke.

Canada.   See No. **522**.

Canterbury New.   See No. **523**.

Cornhill.   See No. **524**.

Cranbrook.   See No. **525**.

Glory to Thee my God this night.   See No. **526**.

162   **An Hymn for Easter Day.**

If   an —gels   sang   a   Sav — ior's   birth   on   that   aus—pi — cious   morn

Printed collections   DIV 2, 3, 4

163 An Hymn for Whitsunday.

He's   come?   Let   ev – 'ry knee   be   bent

Printed collections   DIV 2, 3, 4
Remarks   The style is more soloistic than most congregational hymns, suggesting its use as a sacred song.

164 King's Norton (An Hymn for Good Friday).

No   songs   of   tri – umph now   be   sung

MS 165
Printed collections   DIV 2, 3, 4 / *The English Hymnal with Tunes*, No. 419

165 Kingston (An Hymn for Christmas day).

What   words, what   voi – ces   can   we   bring?

MSS 165, 175
Printed collections   COL 6 / DIV 2, 3, 4 / SEL 2, 3
Remarks   *MS 175* (Lbm Add. 31819) contains a setting for SATB chorus in open score. The melody is in the tenor part, under which an organ accompaniment is written. This setting is probably not by Clarke, as the MS is from late in the eighteenth century, and the only identification, "Jer. Clark," is placed where other pieces in the MS identify the tune of its composer.

My God, my everlasting hope.   The version of No. **166** in *MS 175.*

Nazarene.   See No. **527**

Nottingham.   See No. **170**, St. Magnus.

Our God our Saviour is the Lord.   See No. **528.**

Psalm 11.   See No. **529.**

Psalm 92.   See No. **530.**

Psalm CXVII (Let all the nations of the world).   See No. **169**, St. Magnus.

166 Psalm CXXI ([Brockham] Up to the hills I lift mine eyes).

Up to the hills I lift mine eyes from whence my help

Printed collections   DIV 2, 3, 4
Remarks   The melody appears in later hymnals in various edited versions. It is called "Brockham" in *The English Hymnal with Tunes,* (*ca.* 1906), Nos. 122, 220.

167 Psalm CXLV (I will extol thy sacred name).

I will ex — tol thy sa — cred Name Thou King of Saints

Printed collection   DIV 2

168 Psalm CXLVIII (To laud the heav'nly King).

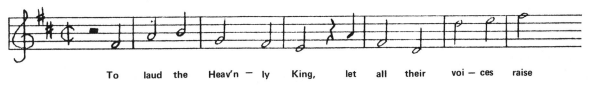

To laud the Heav'n — ly King, let all their voi — ces raise

Printed collections   DIV 2, 3, 4

St. Cecilia's.   See No. **171**, St. Paul's.

169 **St. Magnus** (Birmingham, Nottingham).

MSS   165, 197, 198
Printed collections   ABR 1 / ANC 1 / COL 6 / DIV 2, 3, 4 / PSA 1, 2 / SEL 2 / *The Hymnal 1940,* Nos. 106, 507

St. Nicholas's.   See No. **531** .

170 St. Patrick (Uffingham).

MSS 156, 165

Printed collections ANC 1 / DIV *1*, 2, 3, 4 / PSA 2 / YOU 1 / *The English Hymnal with Tunes,* No. 434

Remarks The version in YOU 1 (The Young . . . companion, 1772-1774) and also in Lbm G.517/11 is slightly altered and ornamented. In both these places, the text starts: "Awake my soul, and with the sun." This is not the same tune or text as No. **160**: "Awake my soul, awake my eyes." The earliest version of the present hymn seems to have the text, "Sleep, downy sleep" as it appears in DIV 1 and DIV 2 (*The Divine Companion,* 1701 and 1707). *MS 156* (Lbm Add. 22099) ascribes the work to a "Mr. Weld" (Weldon?). Ascription to Clarke is assured by DIV 1 and 2.

171 St. Paul's (Bishopthorpe, St. Cecilia's).

Printed collections BLA 1 / COL 6 / PSA 1 / SEL 2 / *The Hymnal 1940,* No. 360

Sleep, downy sleep. See No. **170**.

Sweet is the work. See No. **160**.

172 Tunbridge

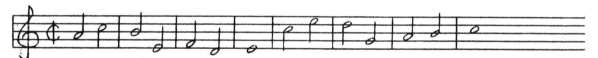

Printed collections DIV *1*, 2, 3, 4 / SAC 3 / *The English Hymnal with Tunes,* No. 88

Uffingham. See No. **170**.

173-199 Reserved for future entries.

ODES

Alexander's feast. See No. **209**.

Barbadoes song. See No. **204**.

200 **Come, come along for a dance and a song** (Music on Henry Purcell's death). 2 rec, 2 ob, 2 tpt, timp, str (Bc). sab/SATB

1 **Overture.** FULL ORCHESTRA

2 **Come, come along.** tpt, timp. a

Come, come a — long come, come a — long come, come a — long

3 **Let monarchs.** str. b

Let mo — narchs in their prov'd imperial seat be — neath

4 **Come, come along.** 2 ob, 2 tpt, timp, str. SATB

Come, come a — long come, come a — long come, come a — long

5 **Sebel.** 2 ob, 2 tpt, str

6 **Hold, shepherds, hold.** 2 ob, str, sb. SATB

Hold, hold, hold shepherds, hold break off your joy

Odes

200—7 The glory of the Arcadian groves. 2 rec. a

The glo — — — — — ry

8 Then break our pipes. 2 ob, str. SATB

Then break our pipes, break our pipes break our pipes

9 And see, Apollo. s

And see, Ap — pol — lo has un — strung

10 Mr. Purcell's farewell. 2 rec, 2 tpt, timp, str

11 All's untuned. 2 ob, 2 tpt, timp, str. SATB

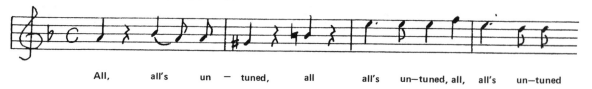

All, all's un — tuned, all all's un—tuned, all, all's un—tuned

12 Antick dance. 2 ob, str

MSS 163, 173

Remarks MS 163 (Lbm Add. 30934) appears to be an autograph. The work was edited by Walter Bergman, and published by B. Schott and Co. in 1961. For further information about the "Sebel" (No. **200.5**) see Thurston Dart, "The Cibell," in *Revue Belge de Musicologie,* 6/no. 1 (1952), 24-30. The article includes discussion of this English dance form with French origins of the period 1690-1710. There is a thematic index and a list of Cibells.

201   **Hail happy queen.**   CHORUS/2 soloists

Remarks   "A new ode being a congratulatory poem on the glorious successes of her Majesty's arms, under the command of the auspicious general his grace the Duke of Marlborough. Set to musick by Mr. Jer. Clark."

1 Hail happy queen.

MUSIC NOT LOCATED

2 Division here will lose its hated name.

MUSIC NOT LOCATED

3 New conquests fill each muse's busie tongue.

MUSIC NOT LOCATED

4 Oh Albion! mark the day that gave her birth.   CHORUS

MUSIC NOT LOCATED

5 Triumph and fame clap their rejoicing wings.   DUET

MUSIC NOT LOCATED

6 Io's shall with repeated Io's join.   CHORUS

MUSIC NOT LOCATED

Printed s. sh. fol.   London, J. Morphew, 1706, in Mc, *Halliwell Collection of Broadsides,* No. 103
Remarks   The page and a half printing of the text is the only source located. The work was "to be perform'd by the best masters, on Friday the 20th of this instant, at seven a clock in Yorkbuildings."

202   **Hark, she's called** (Song on the Assumption).   2 rec, 2 tpt, 2 vln, 2 vla, 2 'celli (Bc).   sab/SATB

1   **Symphony.**   2 tpt, str

2   **Hark, she's called.**   2 vln, 2 rec.   a

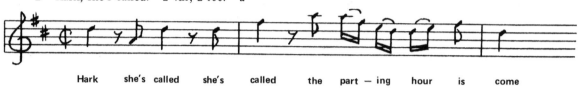

Hark   she's called   she's   called   the   part — ing   hour   is   come

3   **Come away, my love.**   sb

Come come a — way   my   love come a — way come a — way   my   love

3b   **And will she go?**   2 tpt, 2 vln.   ssa

And   will   she   will   she   will   she   goe

4   **Go then, go.**   a

Go   then   go   then   go   glo —   —   —   —   —

5   **Ground.**   2 rec

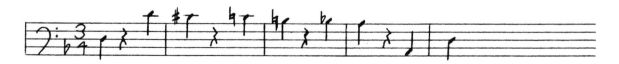

202–6 And while thou go'st. 2 tpt. satb

And   while   thou   go'st   a — long   and   we   will   as

6b Symphony. 2 tpt, str. (Reprise of No. 6)

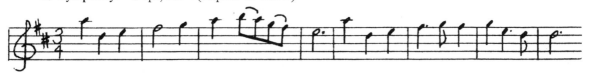

7 Hail, holy Queen of humble hearts. sb, str. SATB

Hail   holy   queen   of   hum — ble   hearts   we   in thy   praise will   give

8 Dance movement. str

9 And though thy dearest. t

And   though   thy   dear — est   thy   dear — est   thy   dear — est

10 Thy sacred name shall be. sab, str. (Reprise)

Thy   sa — cred   name   shall   be   thy   self   to   us   thy   self

11 Maria men and angels sing. FULL ORCHESTRA AND VOICES

Ma — ri — a   men   and   an — gels   sing   Ma — ri — a   mo — ther   of   our   King

MSS   315, *324*

Remarks   *MS 315* (T 1175) is later than *MS 324* (T 1226) and is a collection in various hands on paper with the same watermark. *MS 324* contains odes by Draghi, Purcell, Blow, Clarke, and Carissimi—with varying watermarks and hands throughout.   The watermark of a jester is on the last eight Clarke pages (starting at p. 31), and is most visible on page 31 (fol. 121). It also occurs in the Purcell *Yorkshire Feast* (fol. 69) which is in a different hand (not that of Purcell), and the Draghi *St. Cecilia's Song* (fol. 34) which is in the same hand as the Purcell. The signature at the end: "Jere. Clarke" differs from the one at the beginning of the Ode. The ink changes from black to brown at page 9, but the hand remains the same. The ink change appears to be gradual.

203   **Let Nature smile** (Odes on Queen Ann's Birthday).   2 rec, 2 ob, tpt, timp, str (Bc).   satb/SATB

1 Let Nature smile.   ab

Let   na — ture   smile   Let   na — ture   smile

2 Thou Spring revive.   t

Thou   Spring   re — vive   thou   Spring   re — vive

3 Let Nature smile.   tpt, timp, str.   SATB

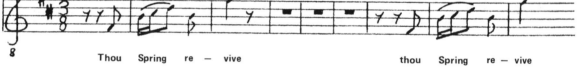

Let   na — ture   smile   let   na — ture   smile

4 Pay your homage.   a, plus 2 rec, 2 ob (rit)

Pay   your   hom — age   cheer — ful   hearts   greet   the   pa — tron — ess   of   arts

5 Shine, thou sun.   sab, plus str (rit)

Shine   thou   sun   shine,   shine,   shine   thou   sun   like   Anna's

203–6 In her brave offspring. a

In her brave off — spring still she'll live nor must she

7 The sun can warm us. 2 vln. b

The sun can warm us

8 Long may great Anna live. tpt, timp, str. SATB

Long may great An—na great Anna live long, long may great

MS 173

Remarks The date of composition is unknown, but obviously must be after 1701, in which year Ann became Queen. The last chorus is incomplete in the manuscript. Stevens breaks off with the note, "Jeremiah Clarke's copy so mutilated and torn, that I was obliged to end my copy in the middle of this grand chorus." Folios 32 and 33 contain the title, "Part of an ode on Queen Ann's Birthday" and the text.

204 No more, great rulers of the sky (Barbadoes Song). 2 tpt, 2 ob, timp, str à 4 (Bc). satb/SATB

1 Overture. FULL ORCHESTRA

2 No more, great rulers of the sky. str. a

No more no more great ru — lers of the sky

204—3 Blest genius of our island. ab, plus str (rit)

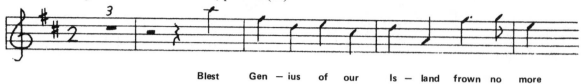

Blest Gen — ius of our Is — land frown no more

4 Behold Apollo and the tuneful nine. ob. a

Be — hold A — pol—lo

5 Musick the darling. sa

Mu — — — — sic mu — — — — — — sic

6 Thus when some hot contagion. 2 tpt, timp, str. SATB

Thus when some hot con — ta — gion of old

7 'Tis done, 'tis done. str. a

8 From this blest time. a

From this blest time no more

9 Annual joy from henceforth. t

An—nual joy from hence forth sing — ing ver — nal sa — cri — fi—ces bring — ing

204–10 Ritornello. str

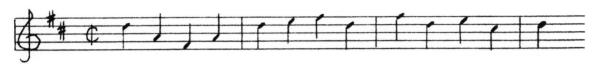

11 Rich wines too that flowing. ab

Rich   wines   too   that   flow — ing   from   pines   that   are

12 Whilst the sun in northern clime. str (b)

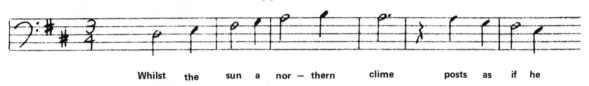

Whilst   the   sun   a   nor — thern   clime   posts   as   if   he

13 Curst with no cold winter here. 2 tpt, timp, str. SATB

Curst   with   no   cold   win — ter   here   Na — ture

MSS Section 1:325 — Sections 1-9:166 — Section 7:200 — Complete:*204*
Remarks All four MSS are from Clarke's time. The signature following *MS 204* (Lcm 1106) indicates that it is possibly an autograph as is surmised in the Lcm Manuscript catalog. After the overture, the *MS 166* (Lbm Add. 31452) copy has the word "Adagio" and then two blank pages before the countertenor solo. This does not appear in *MS 204*, suggesting, along with the relatively neat appearance of the latter, that it is a fair copy for performance from the working copy in the British Museum. A comment at the end of the piece in T 1232 reads: "This piece was compos'd by Mr. Jer. Clarke for ye Gentlemen of ye Island of Barbadoes and performed to them at Stationers Hall." In *MS 200* (Lcm 995), the countertenor aria, "'tis done" is copied in a later hand.

205 Now Albion, raise thy drooping head (Ode on His Majesty's happy Deliverance). 2 rec, 2 ob,
2 tpt, str (Bc). sab/SATB

1 Symphony. 2 tpt, 2 ob, str

205–2 Now Albion, raise thy drooping head. 2 vln. b

Now Al — bion raise thy droo — ping head

3 Our Cesar lives. 2 vln. a

Our Ce — — — sar lives, our Ce — — sar lives

4 Instrumental march. 2 tpt, str

5 Thy sacred life to heaven. 2 rec. s

Thy sa — cred life to heaven so dear

6 Great William lives. tpt. a

Great Wil — liam lives Great _ Wil — liam lives the smi — ling

7 Great William lives. 2 ob, 2 tpt, str. ab/SATB

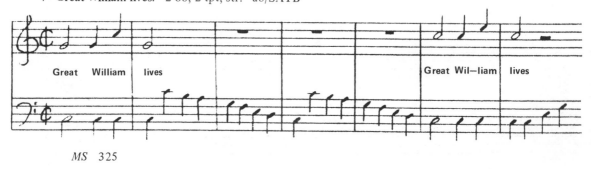

Great William lives   Great Wil—liam lives

MS 325

34

206   **O Harmony, where's now thy power?** (Song on New Year's Day, 1706).   2 rec, str (Bc).   aatb/SATB

1 **Symphony.**   str

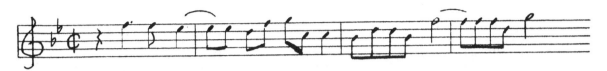

2 **O Harmony, where's now thy power?**   str.   t

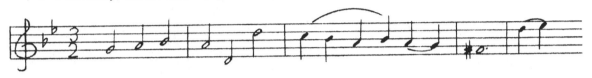

3 **Come, goddess.**   t, plus str/SATB repeat

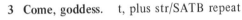

Come god — dess in splen — dor and gran — deur ap—pear to wel — come

4 **A year triumphant.**   vla.   aa

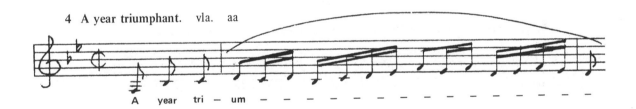

A   year tri — um — — — — — — — —

5 **On pursue your game.**   tb, plus str/SATB (rit)

On pur — sue your game of glo — ry through un — beat — en

6 **No the fruitless chase.**   2 rec.   a/SATB

No no no no the fruit — less chase give our

206 – 7 Oh for a muse of fire. ab, plus str (rit)

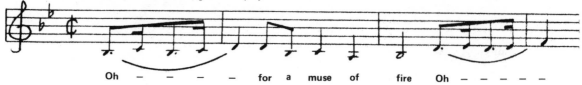

Oh — — — for a muse of fire Oh — — — —

8 Let us try in so glorious a cause. str. SATB

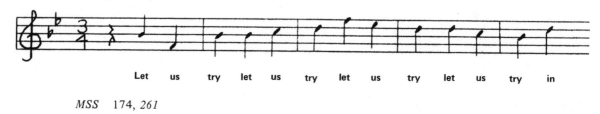

Let us try let us try let us try let us try in

MSS 174, *261*

207 **Pay your thanks** (Ode on the Peace concluded at Ryswick). str (Bc). sab/SATB

1 Pay your thanks. s

Pay your thanks to migh — — — — ty Jove, round his sa — cred

2 Pay your thanks. str. SATB (same text and tune, strings double voices)

Pay your thanks to migh — — — — ty Jove, round his sa — cred

3 Look down, almighty Jove. 2 vln. b (strings have a 21-bar introduction)

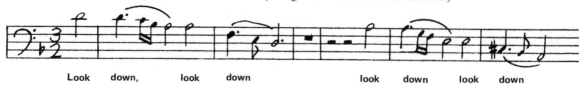

Look down, look down look down look down

4 Ask the oracle. ab/SATB doubled by str (chorus sings a refrain after three verse sections)

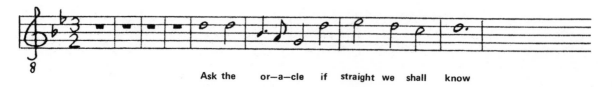

Ask the or—a—cle if straight we shall know

MS 325

Remarks This work was first performed on November 29, 1697 in York Buildings. (*Post Boy,* November 25, 1697). The second performance was on December 16, 1697, along with *Alexander's Feast,* which had been done a few weeks before on St. Cecilia's day. See remarks for No. **208** below.

208 **Tell the World** (Ode on the Peace of Ryswick). 2 ob, 2 tpt, timp, str (Bc). atb/SATB

1 **Overture.** tpt, str

2 **Tell the world.** str. b

Tell the world tell the world tell the world great Ce — sars

2b **Let us rejoyce with instruments of war.** tpt, timp, b (Continuo called "Through")

Let us re — joice with in—stru—ments of war let us re — joice

3 **Come, let us now our voices join.** atb

Come let us now let us now let us now our voi — ces join

4 **Rejoyce, for Europe is at ease.** 2 ob, 2 tpt, str, timp. SATB

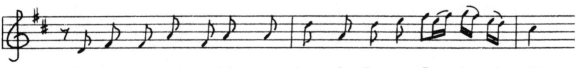

Re — joice re — joice re—joice re — joice for Eu — rope Europe is at ease

MS 325

Remarks The calligrapher of the MS formed his capital "T" in the following manner:
This has caused confusion with earlier writers, who have called the work "O, Tell the world."

On the first page of the piece is written the following: "This piece was composd by Mr. Jer: Clarke upon Ye Peace of Ryswick and prform'd att Drury Lane play house." From this, it seems that "Tell the world" was not the work that was performed at the same time as the third performance of *Alexander's Feast,* since the odes to St. Cecilia were performed in Stationer's Hall. Also, Davey states in his *History of English Music,* p. 341, that on December 16, 1697, " . . . a Pastoral of Clarke's on the Peace of Ryswick was added. This . . . was a task probably more adapted to his tender expressive style than setting the spirit-stirring ode had been." (The ode mentioned is, of course, *Alexander's Feast.*) Since "Tell the World" is a stirring piece, with trumpets and drums, and "Pay your thanks" is in Clarke's tender, minor mode style, Davey was doubtless referring to the latter as the work played with *Alexander's Feast.*

209   **'Twas at the royal feast** (Alexander's Feast).   Text by John Dryden.

MUSIC NOT LOCATED

Remarks   Written and composed for St. Cecilia's Day, 1697.   Performed on November 22 and December 8, 1697, at Hickford's Dancing School for the benefit of the composer and Mr. Roche (*Post Boy,* December 4); and on December 16, 1697, at York Buildings with the addition of No. 207 (*Post Boy*).

Welcome beauty.   See No. **301.**

Remarks   Previously thought of as an ode, this piece is actually the prologue to *The World in the Moon.*

210-299   Reserved for future entries.

THEATRE MUSIC AND SONGS

Entertainments

300   **The Island Princess, Or The Generous Portuguese.**   Made into an opera by Peter Anthony Motteux. Music by Jeremiah Clarke, Richard Leveridge, Daniel Purcell. 1699.   Clarke's portions are:

A   Incidental instrumental music.   str

1   Overture.

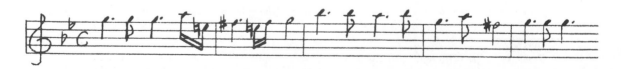

300A—2 Sebell.

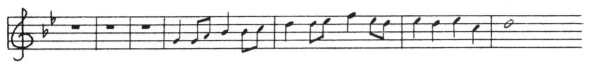

3 Roundo—Fourth Act Tune.

4 Eg [*sic*] Dance.

5 Spring Dance.

6 Round O Minuet.

7 First Act Tune.

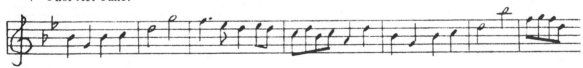

8 First Musick.

300A—9 Second Musick.

10 First Musick.

11 Second Musick.

12 Third Act Tune.

300B Mourn, ye drooping seat of Pleasures (The Four Seasons. An Interlude).   2 tpt, timp, str (Bc).
sssaatb/SATB

1 Sinfonia.   tpt, timp, str

2 Mourn, mourn.   2 vln.   b/SATB

Mourn   mourn   droo — ping   feet   of   plea — sures   mourn

(1) Repeat of **Sinfonia "Gay March."**   tpt, timp, str

300B–3 Rouze, ye tuneful sons of art. a

Rouze   ye tune — ful   sons ye tune — ful tune—ful   sons

4 Revive every pleasure. ab, plus chorus reprise

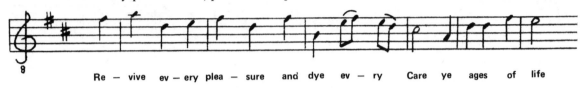

Re — vive ev—ery plea — sure and dye ev — ry   Care ye ages of life

5 Must I a girl forever be. ss. See No. **376.**

Must   I   a   girl for ev—er be,   will   ne'er my Mo — ther mar—ry me

6 Spring Dance. str

6a Oh why thus alone. s. **MUSIC NOT EXTANT**

7 Dialogue between a Gent and a Country Lass ('Tis sultry weather). sb. See No. **378.**

'Tis   sultry   wea — ther pret—ty   maid,   'tis sul — — try

8 Summer Dance by Blacks. str

300B–9   Dialogue between a widow and a rake (Oh my poor husband).   ab.   See No. **377**.

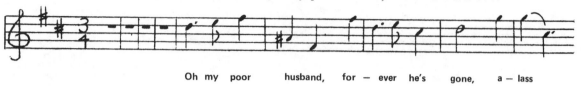

Oh my poor   husband,   for — ever he's   gone,   a — lass

10   Autumn Dance by a French clown and Country Woman in wooden shoes.   str

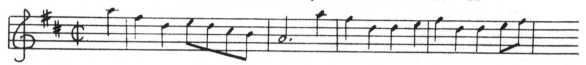

11   Dialogue between four people (Hold, good Mr. Fumble).   sssb

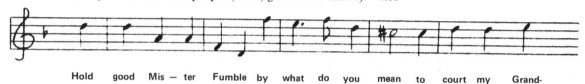

Hold   good   Mis — ter   Fumble   by   what   do   you   mean   to   court   my   Grand-

12   Winter Dance with a stove, a Dutch woman with an old miser.   str

13   Come all, let soft desire your heart engage.   s

Come   all,   come   all,   come   all,   come   all

14   Hail, god of desire.   tpt, str.   SATB (includes a grand dance and a short verse, then the main chorus reprise)

300C   Epilogue (Now to you, ye dry wooers).   ss.   See No. **355**.

Now   to   you   ye   dry   Woo — ers   Old   Beaus   and   no

MSS Section A:*205* — Section B:*150* (also includes No. **438**–"Second Act Tune") — Section B.5: 22 — Section B.7:266

Printed collections Section A.2:THE 2 — Section A.6:THE 1 — Section B.5:TWE 1 — Section B.7: COL 7 — Section B.8:THE 2 — Section B.9:COL 7 / TWE 1 — Section B.10:THE 2 — Section B.12: THE 2 — Section C:COL 7 / WIT 8, 15 / Three dances:THE 2

Printed s. sh. fol. Section B.5:Ckc 110.22. Ref., No. 78; Eu S^x 17.25 (88) — Section B.7:Lbm G.304, fols. 160v-161; Lbm G.312, fol. 10; Eu S^x 17.25 (132); Ckc 110.22. Ref., No. 112 — Section B.9:Lbm G.304, fols. 117v-118; Eu S^x 17.25 (101); Lbm H.1601, fols. 340v-341; Mc Halliwell, 1402; SMh (Huth) 81013.V.17-18

Remarks MS 150 (Lbm Add. 15318) is said to be an autograph by the Lbm catalog. This is doubtful according to Christopher Powell, the hand is probably that of "JK"–the copyist of the Drury Lane Theatre. According to Michael Tilmouth, *A Calendar of References to Music in Newspapers Published in London and the Provinces (1660-1719)*, London, 1961, *The Island Princess* was first performed for the public on November 14, 1702. It then received subsequent performances in 1706: January 8, 9, 10, 11, 15, 17, 18, 31; February 7; March 7, 16; April 18; December 10, 18. In 1707: November 29. In 1708: January 3. In 1715: January 25, 27, 28, 29; February 8, 19. A copy of the printed play may be found in the Newberry Library (Chicago): Case Y, 135, M 8573 + 4. This publication contains a number of requests for musical insertions, which do not account for all the music extant for the play. The following comment at the end of the printed play suggests that not all the music listed here was performed for any one staging of the play. It also gives evidence that Clarke's entertainment was perhaps originally designed to be inserted in an earlier production, and perhaps in a different play: "The Four Seasons, or Love in every Age. A Musical Interlude. Set to Musick by Mr. Jeremy Clarke." "This entertainment is performed at the end of the last Act, but was design'd for another season, and another occasion: and what is mark'd (   ) is omitted" (Peter Motteux, *The Island Princess* . . .). The final epilogue in this publication has no reference to music, and so the epilogue (No. **300C**) was presumably for the earlier performance. For reference concerning the "Sebell" (Section A.2), see the remarks under No. **201**.

301   **The World in the Moon.**   By Elkanah Settle. Music by Jeremiah Clarke and Daniel Purcell. Clarke's portions are:

A   **Prologue** (Welcome Beauty, all the charms).   tpt, str (Bc).   satb/ATB?

1 Overture.   tpt, str

2 Welcome Beauty, all the charms.   str.   a

Wel — come beauty   wel—come wel—come   wel—come beauty

3 If the Fates that rule below.   atb

If   the   fates that   rule   be — low   all   are   smi — — — — — ing

301A – 4 Smile then with a beam divine. s, str reprise. See No. **361**.

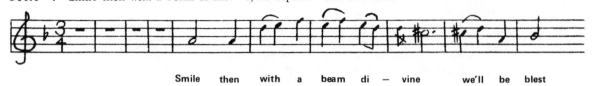

Smile then with a beam di — vine we'll be blest

5 Your graces let the muses share. s

Your gra — ces let the Mu — ses share

6 In all your quiver. 2 vln. atb (or ATB?)

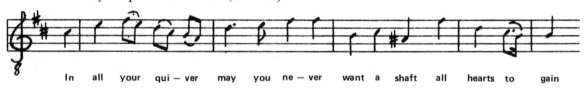

In all your qui — ver may you ne — ver want a shaft all hearts to gain

301B Entertainment after the First Act (Within this happy world above). 2 rec, tpt, str (Bc). sab/SATB

1 Symphony. 2 rec, str. a

2 Within this happy world above. 2 rec, str. a

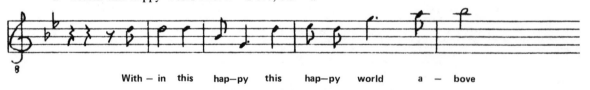

With — in this hap—py this hap—py world a — bove

3 Divine Astrea hither flew. s, plus str/SATB reprise. See No. **339**.

Di — vine Astre — a hither flew to Cynthi — a's

301B—4 Sound, sound the trumpet. tpt. a (bass missing from MS, added by R. Stevens)

Sound sound sound sound sound the trum — pet

5 **Soft peace on earth.** str. b (viola missing)

Soft – – – – – – – – – – – – peace on earth

6 **While thus our calmer pleasures.** ab. See No. **369.**

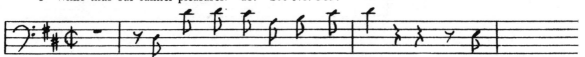

While thus our calm—er plea — sures flow

7 **Trumpets rattle.** tpt, str. SATB

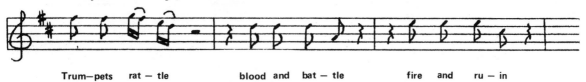

Trum—pets rat — tle blood and bat — tle fire and ru — in

8 **A Dance of Four Swans.** str

9 **A Dance for Green Men.** str

MSS Section A.4:355 — Section B.6:326, 355 — Complete:174

Printed collections Section A.4:WOR 1, 2 — Section B.3:COL 7 / SON 4 / WIT 3, 7, 8, 15 / WOR 1, 2 — Section B.6:WOR 2

Printed s. sh. fol. Section B.3:Lbm G.304, fol. 47 — Section B.6:Lg 313, fol. 9

Remarks Performed July 1, 1697 (*Post Boy*) and May 24, 1698 (*Post Boy*). Single songs that received separate publication are also entered under Solo Songs. In *MS 174* (Lbm Add. 31813) the prologue is on folios 99-106v, the Entertainment after the First Act is on folios 107-121, and the Entertainment after the Second Act, which is by Daniel Purcell, is on folios 121v-126. The song, "I seek no more to shady coverts," (see No. **348)** was also written for the play but is not part of these Entertainment Sections.

302-309   Reserved for future entries.

Instrumental Music for the Theatre

---

310   **All for the Better.**   Mr. Jer. Clarkes Aires in the Comedy call'd **All for the Better.**

1   **Overture.**

2   **Gavott.**   See No. **455.**

3   **Hornpipe Round O.**   See No. **456.**

4   **Aire.**

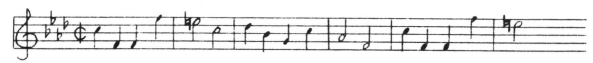

5   **Round O.**

6   **Aire.**   See No. **450.**

310–7   **Farwell.**   See No. **454.**

8   **Aire.**

9   **Minuet Round O.**

MSS   Complete: 281 – Section 5: 285 (T & B only)

Printed collection   HAR 1

Printed s. sh. fol.   Lbm d.24. (12.), imperfect; Lbm H.313, imperfect

Remarks   The order of individual pieces as listed here is taken from HAR 1 (Harmonia Anglicana, 1702). In *MS 281* (Och 3) the "Round O" (Section 5) and second "Aire" (Section 6) are reversed. Section 3 is an ensemble version of the harpsichord piece No. **456.** Section 6 is an ensemble version of the harpsichord piece No. **450.** Section 7 is an ensemble version of the harpsichord piece No. **454.**

311   **Anthony and Cleopatra.**   From a play of the same name by Sir Charles Sedley, 1677.   str

1   **Overture.**   str

2   **Lady Warton's Faerwell.**   str

MS   205

Remarks   Other songs and instrumental pieces which Clarke is reported to have set for this play have not been located.

The Island Princess.   Twelve pieces for strings à 4.   See No. **300A.**

312   **Mr. Clarke's Tunes in ye Opera** _____.   Ten untitled tunes in D major and minor.

312–8

9

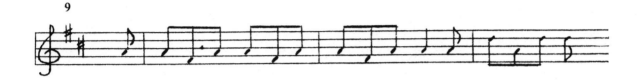

10

MS 180

313   **Titus Andronicus.**   From **Titus Andronicus, Or The Rape of Lavinia**, adapted by Edward Ravenscroft, 1687.   str

1   **Overture.**   str

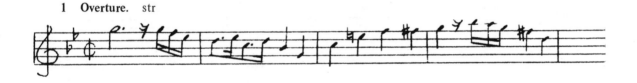

2   **Dance movement.**   str (probably an Act Tune)

MS 205

314   **The Vertuous Wife.**   From **The Virtuous Wife, Or Good Luck at Last**, by Thomas Durfey, revived 1696-1697.   Nine tunes in C major and minor, D major and minor, and G minor.

1

314–2

MS 180

Remarks See W. Thorp, *Songs from the Restoration Theatre*, pp. 36-37, 98-99.

315   **A Wife for Any Man.**   Mr. Clark's First Trebles in ye Farce called **A Wife for Any Man**, by
Thomas D'Urfey, 1695-1697.   Nine tunes in G major and minor.

315–8

9

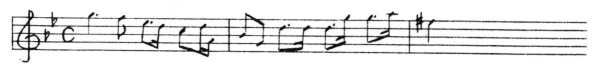

MS   180, 205

316   **Music for an Unnamed Play.**

1   Overture Mr. Jer^e: Clark.

2   Unnamed Act Tune.

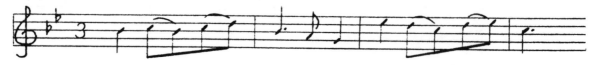

3   Unnamed Act Tune.

[♩.]

4   Unnamed Act Tune.

5   Unnamed Act Tune.

316–6   Unnamed Act Tune.

7   Grave.

8   Unnamed Act Tune.

MS 265

Remarks   First treble on pages 1-3 of *MS 265* (Ob Ms. Mus. Sch. C.73); second treble on pages 25-27; and Continuo on pages 47-49.

317-329   Reserved for future entries.

Solo Songs

This section includes both theatrical songs and those not connected with the theatre.
Individual songs from larger works such as entertainments and odes are included only
if they received separate publication, in which case, they are given a separate catalog number.
Each song is put into one of the following categories according to use or musical characteristics.

E — Entertainment in the theatre, not part of the play
G — For general use, not connected with the theatre
P — Written into the play by the playwright
S — Scotch song

330   A gentle warmth comes o're my heart (A new song).   D minor.   **G**

Printed collection   COL 7

331 **Ah Charmion.** Song sung at the Theatre Royal. Set by Mr. Clarke. G minor. **E**

Ah! Ah! Char — mi—on ah! ah — — — — — —

Printed s. sh. fol. Lg 313, fol. 7 ("exactly engrav'd by Tho. Cross," [London, *ca.* 1703])

332 **Ah fly.** E minor. **G**

Ah! fly ah fly, fly, fly

Printed collection COL 7
Printed s. sh. fol. Lbm G.304, fol. 10 (London, *ca.* 1705); Eu collection, item 5

333 **Alas, alas here lies the poor Alonzo slain.** Sung by Mrs. Hodgson in the Play call'd *Timon of Athens*, by Thomas Shadwell, 1677.

A — lass, a — lass here lies the poor A—lon—zo

Printed collection MON 1
Printed s. sh. fol. Ob Mus. 1 c.73, fol. 63

334 **Cease that inchanting song.** A song on a lady's singing set to Musick by Mr. Clarke. C minor. **G**

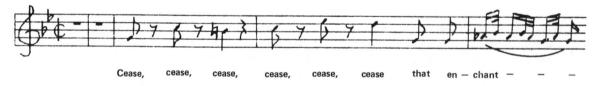

Cease, cease, cease, cease, cease, cease that en — chant — — —

Printed s. sh. fol. Lg 313, fol. 8 (London: Cross, *ca.* 1703); Lcm II.B.2, fol. 36 (same engraving)

335 **Celia is soft.** A song . . . sung by Mrs. Erwin at the Theater Royall. G minor. **E**

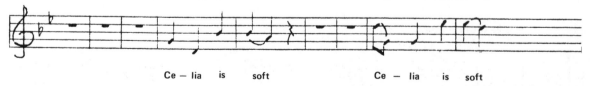

Ce — lia is soft Ce — lia is soft

MS 22
Printed collection MER 1
Printed s. sh. fol. Ckc 110.22. Ref. No. 20; Eu S^x 17.25 (28); Lbm H.1600, fol. 102 (London, *ca.* 1700); Lbm K.7.i.2, fol. 102 (same); Mc Halliwell (same)

336   **Come, sweet lass** (a national English song).   G major.   **G**

Come sweet   lass   this   bon — ny   wea — ther   Let's   to — ge — ther   come

MSS   156, 157, 167, 280
Printed collections   WIT 1, 4, 10, 14
Remarks   This song was used in the production of *The Beggar's Opera* by Mr. Gay, Act 3, London, 1728. See also Claude Simpson, *The British Broadside Ballad*, pp. 127-128, and William Chappell, *The Ballad Literature and Popular Music of the Olden Time*, Vol. 2, pp. 600-601.

337   **Cou'd a Man be secure.**   From *The Committee*, by Sir Robert Howard, revived 1699.   A new song . . . sung by Mr. Leveridge.   B flat major.   **E**

Could   a   man   be   se — cure   that   life   would   en — dure

Printed collections   COL 7 / SEL 4
Printed s. sh. fol.   Lbm G.304, fol. 33; Ob Mus. 1 c.73 (42); Lbm G.307, fol. 18; Hamburg Sull B-102; W Fol: Songs, 8883,44; Ge N.b.10, fol. 3.

The Country Farmer.   See No. **342.**

338   **De'll take the wars.**   C major.   B.   **S**

De'll   take   the   wars   that   hurried   Willy   from me   who to   love me

MS   157
Printed collections   SEL 4 / SON 1 / WIT 1, 4, 10, 12
Remarks   This tune is said to be in the play, *A Wife for Any Man* (see index to *MS 205*) and reappears in *The Lover's Opera* by Chetwood as "The Cheering sun shall cease," p. 13. Some doubt is cast upon the attribution of the work to Clarke by the Playford 1696 broadside in Chetham's Library (No. 2058), which ascribes the tune to Charles Powell. See Simpson: *The British Broadside*, p. 178.

339   **Divine Astrea hither flew.**   A song in *The World in the Moon*, sung by Mrs. Cross, . . . in Entertainment after Act 1.

Di — vine   As-tre—a   hi — ther flew   to   Cyn—thi — a's

MS   174
Printed collections   COL 7 / WIT 3, 7, 8, 15 / WOR 1, 2
Printed s. sh. fol.   Lbm G.304, fol. 47

340 Farewell ungrateful nymph, farewell. bc. **S**

Fare — well un — grate — ful nymph, fare—well

Printed collection MER 1

341 Hail, happy Britain. bc. ab (From his own copy in an old book of his.)

MS 267

Remarks This work has been located only in this one mid-eighteenth century copy. In order to assure us of its authenticity, someone has written "from his own copy in an old book of his." Without the original, there is some doubt as to authenticity.

342 Hark, the Cock crow'd, Or The Country Farmer. Text by Thomas D'Urfey. C major. **G, P**

Hark the cock crow'd, tis day all a—broad, and looks like a jol—ly

MSS 155, 156, 174, 266
Printed collections COL 7 / SON 1 / WIT 1, 2, 4, 5, 10, 12
Printed s. sh. fol. Lbm G.304, fol. 67; Lbm G.305, fol. 56; Lbm H.1601, fol. 195; Eu S^x 17.25, fol. 51; Ob Mus. 1 c.73, fol. 35; Ckc (110.22. Ref.) No. 46; SMh (Huth) 81013.V.64
Remarks This tune was later used several times, fitted with different texts as follows:
  1728 — "My sorrows are passed," in *Penelope*. The last song. Printed in Lbm 80.c. 23/3, p. 59, and appendix.
  1729 — "A Guardian commands," in *Momus turn'd fabulist*. London, 1729, p. 13.
  1729 — "As virtue from hence was banished," in *The Patron*, by Odell. First song.
  1729 — "The World's a deceit," in *The Village Opera*, by Johnson. Printed in Lcm II.G.2.
  1730 — "Such wretched poor elves," in *The Lovers Opera*, by Chetwood, p. 33.
  1734 — "When a lover like you," in *The Intriguing Chambermaid*, by Fielding. Printed in Lcm II.G.2, and SMh.

343 How often have I curst that sable deceit. A major. **G**

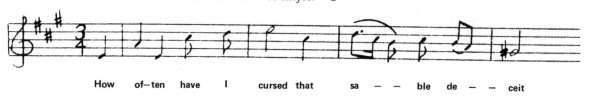

How of—ten have I cursed that sa — — ble de — — ceit

Printed collections WIT 8, 15
Printed s. sh. fol. Mc Halliwell, fol. 1758 (exactly engrav'd by Tho: Cross)

344   I'm vex'd to think.   D minor.   **G**

I'm   vex'd   to   think   that   Da — mon   wooed me,   who   with   sight

MSS   167, 174
Printed collections   WIT 11, 16
Printed s. sh. fol.   Lcm II.B.2, fol. 37 (Tho: Cross, *ca.*1703)

345   I'm wounded by Amanda's Eyes.   C minor – C major.   **G**

I'm   wound — — — — ed

Printed collection   MER 1

346   In faith 'tis true I am in Love.   (Tune only)   **G**

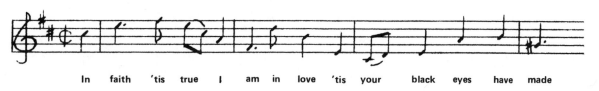

In   faith   'tis   true   I   am   in   love   'tis   your   black   eyes   have   made

Printed collection   WIT 4

347   I seek no more to shady coverts.   From *The World in the Moon,* by Elkanah Settle, 1697.   Sung by
Mrs. Temple.   E minor.   **E, S**

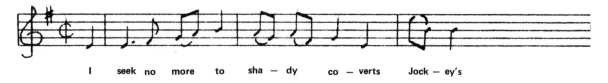

I   seek   no   more   to   sha — dy   co — verts   Jock — ey's

MSS   22, 174
Printed collections   COL 4, 5, 7 / WIT 3, 7, 8, 16
Printed s. sh. fol.   Lbm G.309, fol. 54; Lcm II.B.2, fol. 32; Eu S^x 17.25, fol. 68 (*ca.*1697)
Remarks   This is not part of the Entertainment, No. **301,** but occurs elsewhere in the play.

348 If you'd win Mellissa's heart. bc. **G**

Printed collection MER 1

349 Jockey was a dawdy lad. From *The Campaigners,* by Thomas D'urfey, 1698. Sung by Miss Campion. D minor. **P, S**

MS 266
Printed collections COL 5 / SON 1 / WIT 1, 4, 10, 12
Printed s. sh. fol. Eu S^X 17.25, fol. 62 (*ca.*1698); Lbm I.530, fol. 27 (Tho. Cross, *ca.*1698)
Remarks This work is falsely attributed to a Mr. Wilkins in COL 2 (A collection of . . .
songs . . . , *ca.*1732).

350 Jockey was as brisk and blith a lad. Sung by Mrs. Cross. C major. **E, S**

MSS 156, 167, 266
Printed collections COL 4, 5, 7 / SON 3 / THE 1 / WIT 1, 4, 10, 14
Printed s. sh. fol. Eu S^X 17.25, fol. 66; Lbm G.309, fol. 56; Lcm II.B.2, fol. 34; Wc; Ws
Remarks In *MS 156* (Lbm Add. 22099), the work is called "Shore's Trumpet." THE 1 (Theater
Musick . . . 1698) calls the piece "Round O Mr. Clarke. Mr. Shor's Trumpet Tune." See No. **434.**

351 Kneel, Oh kneel. From *Cinthia and Endimion,* by Thomas D'Urfey, 1696. Sung by Mrs. Temple. G minor. **E**

Printed s. sh. fol. Lcm II.A.32, fol. 10 (Tho. Cross)

352 **Long has Pastora rul'd the plain.**   From *The Relapse, Or Virtue in Danger,* by Sir John Vanbrugh, 1696. Sung by Miss Campion at the Theater in Dorset Garden.   G minor. **E**

Long — — — has Pa — sto — ra rul'd — — — the plain

MS 22

Printed collection ALA 1

Printed s. sh. fol. Lg 313, fol. 6 (Tho. Cross, *ca.* 1702); Lbm G.316.n, fol. 16 (sold by Henry Playford); Eu S^X 17.25, fol. 78; Ob Mus. Sch. c.97, fol. 12 (Playford, *ca.* 1700)

353 **Lord, what's come to my mother?**   From *The Bath, Or The Western Lass,* by T. D'Urfey, 1701. Sung by Mrs. Lucas.   G major. **E**

Lord what's come to my Moth — er that ev — ery day more than o — thers

MSS 174, 266

Printed collections COL 7 / CON 1 / SEL 1 / SON 1 / WIT 6, 9, 12

Printed s. sh. fol. Lbm G.304, fol. 92; Lbm G.310, fol. 21; Lbm H.1601, fol. 289 (*ca.* 1705); Ckc (110.22. Ref.) No. 70; SMh (Huth) 81013.IV.49 (London, *ca.* 1705); Hamburg SuUB; Eu S^X 17.25 (76) (*ca.* 1702); Mc Halliwell, fol. 1469; Wc; Ws, Songs 888E, 144

Remarks In SEL 1 (Select Lessons . . . , 1702) this song is called "The Western Lass A Country Dance."

354 **Now that Love's holiday is come** (A song on a wedding).   G minor. **G**

Now that Love's ho — li — day has come and Magg the Maid hath swept

Printed collections WIT 4, 14

Remarks Twenty stanzas are included in WIT 14 (Wit and Mirth, Vol. 3). There is an alternate poem to the same tune on page 109: "He that intends to take a wife."

355 **Now to you, ye dry wooers.**   Epilogue from *The Island Princess,* by Peter Anthony Motteux, 1699. Sung by Mrs. Lindsey and the Boy.   D major. **P** (Epilogue)   See No. **300C.**

Now to you yee dry Woo — ers old Beaus and no

Printed collections COL 7 / WIT 8, 15

Printed s. sh. fol. Lg 313, fol. 10 (London, T. Cross, *ca.* 1705); Mc Halliwell, fol. 1953 (T. Cross, *ca.* 1705)

356 **Oh! I feel the mighty Dart.** Bc. **G**

Oh!   Oh!   Oh!   I feel the migh — —

Printed collection   MER 1

357 **Serene and gentle was the air.**

COPY MISSING FROM Lbm

Printed collection   MER 1

358 **Silvia by a double charm.** C minor. **G**

Sil — via   by a   dou — ble   charm, a double charm — — — —

Printed collection   MER 1

359 **Slaves to London I'll deceive you.** From *The Comical Mistakes, Or Love's a Jest,* by Peter Anthony Motteux, 1696. Sung by Mr. Lee. C major. **P** (Act 1, scene 1)

Slaves to London I'll de — ceive you, for the coun—try, now I leave

Printed collections   WIT 9, 12, 15
Printed s. sh. fol.   Lbm G.315, fol. 111 (T. Cross)

360 **Sleep betray'd the unhappy lover.** **G**

Sleep   be — tray'd the unhap — — py lov—er

Printed collection   MER 1

361 **Smile then with a beam Divine.** From *The World in the Moon,* by Elkanah Settle, 1697. Sung by Mrs. Cross. D minor. **P** (Prologue, Verse 3) See No. **301A.4.**

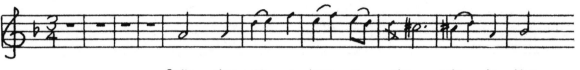

Smile then with a beam di — vine we'll be blest

MSS 174, 355
Printed collections WOR 1, 2
Printed s. sh. fol. Lg 313, fol. 11

362 **So sweet's the charms of love.** From *Madam Fickle, Or The Witty False One,* by Thomas D'Urfey, revived 1691. Sung by Mrs. Lucas. A major. **E**

So sweet's the charms of love so sweet's the thoughts to en—joy

Printed s. sh. fol. Lcm II.A.32, fol. 6

363 **The bonny grey-ey'd morn.** From *The Fond Husband,* by Thomas D'Urfey, a revival 1697. Sung by Mrs. Willis. **E, S**

The bon—ny grey — ey'd morn be — gan to peep, when

MSS 156, 174, 179
Printed collections SEL 4 / SON 3 / WIT 1, 2, 4, 5, 10, 14
Printed s. sh. fol. Lbm G.304, fol. 151; Lbm G.316, fol. 38; Lcm II.A.32.(8.); CDp M.C.2. 38 (8); Ob Mus. 1 c.118 (24); Ge N.b.23 (9)
Remarks This song was used in the production of the Scotch ballad opera, *Patie and Peggy,* by T. C., Act 1, London, 1730. It was also used in the production of the ballad opera, *The Beggar's Opera,* by Mr. Gay, Act 1, scene 2, London, 1728.

364 **The rosey morn lukes blith and gay.** From *Love at First Sight,* by David Crawford, 1704. G major. **E, S**

The ro — sey morn lukes bleeth and gay

MS 174
Printed collections COL 4, 5 / MON 1 / WIT 11, 16
Printed s. sh. fol. Lbm G.312, fol. 49 (*ca.*1720); Lbm H.1601, fol. 470 (*ca.*1710); Mc Halliwell 1550 and 1901

365 **Was it a dream?** A song in the second part of *The Fool in Fashion,* by Colley Cibber, 1695. Sung by Mrs. Linsey.

Was it a dream or did I hear the god — dess at whose feet I lye

Printed s. sh. fol. Ob Mus. 1 c.73 (24)

366 **What shall I do? I've lost my heart.** bc. **G**

What shall I do? I've lost my heart

MS 22
Printed collection MER 1

367 **When maids live to thirty.** From *The Cornish Comedy,* Act 2, by George Powell, *ca.*1696. Sung by Mr. Leveredge. G minor. **P** (Act 2, scene 1)

When maids live to thirty yet ne — ver re — pent — ed

MS 174
Printed collections SON 4 / WIT 6, 9, 15
Printed s. sh. fol. Lbm G.316.g, fol. 71 (*ca.*1710); Lbm H.1606, fol. 486 (*ca.*1698); Ws; Wc; Mc Halliwell, 1970 (*ca.*1700); Lcm II.A.32, fol. 9 (Tho. Cross); Lcm II.B.2, fol. 31 (Walsh and Hare); Ckc (110.22. Ref.) No. 135; SMh (Huth) 81013.III.18 (*ca.*1698)
Remarks See Claude Simpson, *The British Broadside Ballad,* p. 763.

368 **While the lover is thinking.** From *The Amorous Miser,* Act 3, by Peter Anthony Motteux, 1705. C major. **P**

While the lov — er is think — ing with my friend I'll be drink — ing

MSS 174, 177 (melody only)
Printed collections SON 4 / WIT 3, 7, 8, 15

369 **Whilst thus our calmer pleasures flow.** From *The World in the Moon,* by Elkanah Settle, 1697. A duet sung by Mr. Leveridge and Mr. Freeman. D major. **E** See No. **301B.6.**

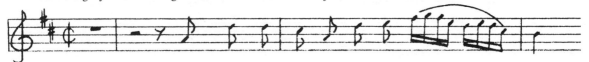

Whilst thus our calm — er plea — sures flow   flow

MSS 326, 355
Printed collection WOR 2
Printed s. sh. fol. Lg 313, fol. 9 (Cross, *ca.* 1702)

370 **Why does Willy shun his dear.** A Scotch song sung by Mrs. Cross at the theatre. F major. **E, S**

Why does Wil—ly shun his dear, why is he ne — ver here

MS 167
Printed collections COL 4, 5 / SON 3 / WIT 1, 4, 10, 14
Printed s. sh. fol. Lbm G.313, fol. 68 (*ca.* 1710)

371 **Young Corydon and Phyllis sate.** G minor. **G**

Young Co — ry — don and Phyl — lis sate in a love—ly grove

Printed collections CON 1 / SON 4 / WIT 9, 15
Printed s. sh. fol. Lbm G.304, fol. 190 (*ca.* 1695); Lbm G.305, fol. 9 (*ca.* 1710); Lbm H.1601, fol. 538 (*ca.* 1705); Lbm 11621.i.1 (86.); Lcm II.A.20, fol. 18; Lcm II.B.2, fol. 17; Mc Halliwell, fol. 1643; SMh (Huth) 81013.V.53 (*ca.* 1705)
Remarks This tune was later fitted to the text, "My rage is past conceiving," in the opera *Silvia,* printed in 1731 (Act 2, scene 16). Copies are to be found in Lcm II.G.2, p. 49, and SMh.

372-374 Reserved for future entries.

Dialogues

---

375 **If Cloris please.** From *The Cornish Comedy,* by George Powell, 1696. Text by Mr. Hanes. Music by Clarke. **NOT EXTANT.** In two parts, following Acts 2 and 3. See No. **379.**

Printed plays CHn; Wc (2); Ws

376 **Must I a girl forever be.** A dialogue between Miss Campion and Mr. Magnus's Boy, from *The Four Seasons,* a musical interlude in *The Island Princess,* by Peter Motteux, 1699. See No. **300B.5.**

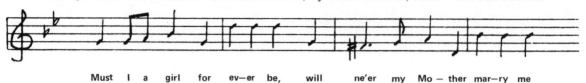

Must I a girl for ev—er be, will ne'er my Mo—ther mar—ry me

MSS 22, 150
Printed collection TWE 1
Printed s. sh. fol. Ckc (110.22.Ref.) No. 78; Eu S^x 17.25, fol. 88

377 **Oh, my poor husband.** A dialogue between a widow and a rake. From *The Four Seasons* . . . See No. **300B.9.**

Oh my poor hus—band, for ev—er he's gone, a — lass

MS 150
Printed collections COL 7 / TWE 1
Printed s. sh. fol. Lbm G.304, fols. 117v-118 (*ca.*1705); Eu S^x 17.25, fol. 101 (*ca.*1705); Lbm H.1601, fols. 340v-341 (*ca.*1700); Mc Halliwell, fol. 1402; SMh (Huth) 81013.V.17-18

378 **'Tis sultry weather.** From *The Four Seasons* . . . See No. **300B.7.**

'Tis sultry wea — ther pret—ty maid, 'tis sul — try

MS 266
Printed collection COL 7
Printed s. sh. fol. Lbm G.304, fols. 160v-161 (*ca.*1705); Lbm G.312, fol. 10 (*ca.*1705); Eu S^x 17.25, fol. 132 (*ca.*1705); Ckc (110.22.Ref.) No. 112

379 **Well Chloris how find you.** A Dialogue between Mr. James Bowen and Mrs. Cross in *The Cornish Comedy.*

Well Chlor — is how find you your self

Printed s. sh. fol. Ob Mus. 2 c.76 (1) (Tho. Cross, *ca.*1700)

Whilst thus our calmer pleasures flow. A duet rather than a dialogue, therefore placed with the solo songs which are in the same style. See No. **369.**

Occasional Songs

380 Drink, my boys, drink (Young Gustavus, Or the King of Sweden's Health).   Dedicated to all the Swedish Merchants in London.   To a March of Mr. Jeremy Clark's.   See No. **433**.

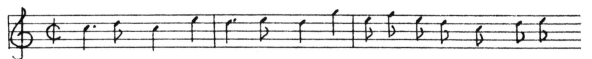

Tho 'tis clear, his sneak — ing here, was fly — ing to be taught of us

MS 22
Printed collections   COL 7 / SON 2 / WIT 3, 7, 8, 13
Printed s. sh. fol.   Eu S^X 17.24, fol. 32

381 Each tender Virgins fears will fly away (A song on the siege of Barcelona).

Each ten — der vir — gins fears will fly a — way

Printed s. sh. fol.   Lg 313, fol. 12 (Tho. Cross, *ca.* 1702)

382 Twelve hundred years at least (A song on ye annual feast of St. George).   Tune also used as a Serenade for harpsichord.   See No. **437**.

Twelve hun—dred years at least has St. George been our pro — tec — tor

Printed collection   COL 7
Printed s. sh. fol.   Lbm G.304, fol. 142; Eu S^X 17.25, fol. 120

383 Ulm is gon, but basely won (A Health to the Imperialists, Or an Invective Ode on the Treachery of the Elector of Bavaria).   Text by Thomas D'Urfey.   Tune also used as a keyboard March, No. **433**, and the song, "Drink, my boys, drink," No. **380**.

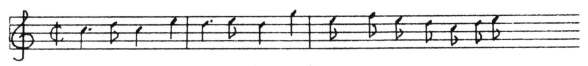

Ulm is gon, but base — ly won, and treach — er —ous Ba — var — i — a

Printed collections   COL 7 / SON 2 / WIT 8, 13
Printed s. sh. fol.   Lbm G.304, fol. 165 (1702); Eu S^X 17.25, fol. 139

384 Whilst the French their arms discover (Ode on the Union of the King and Parliament, 1700).
Text by Thomas D'Urfey.   Tune also used as King William's March, No. **432**.

Whilst   the   French   their   arms dis — cov—er   by   the   troops   a — broad

MS   174
Printed collections   COL 7 / SON 2 / WIT 3, 7, 8, 13
Printed s. sh. fol.   Lbm G.304, fol. 171 (1701); Eu S^X 17.25 (144)

Young Gustavus, Or the King of Sweden's Health. Dedicated to all the Swedish Merchants in London.
See No. **380**.

385 An Elegy on the . . . Death of . . . J. C. . . .   (Weep all ye Swains, weep . . .)   By Richard Brown.

Weep   all   ye   Swains,   Weep

Printed s. sh. fol.   Mc Halliwell, 1583 (London, *ca.* 1708)
Remarks   These songs, Nos. **385** and **386**, are clearly not by Clarke, but are included in this
catalog due to the rare human reference to Clarke and his dog, made by a fellow composer.

386 On Mr. Jere Clarks old dogg Spott. By Richard Brown.

The   Pro — phets   Old   Dog   was   a   man — ner — ly   Curr

Printed collections   JOV 1 (1709) / MON 1 (1706 and 1708)
Printed s. sh. fol.   Mc Halliwell, fol. 1388
Remarks   See remarks under No. **385**.

387-389   Reserved for future entries.

Catches

390 Here's a health to the King.   Three equal voices

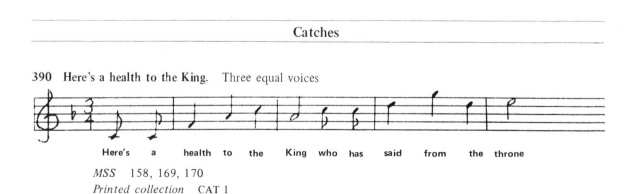

Here's   a   health   to   the   King   who   has   said   from   the   throne

MSS   158, 169, 170
Printed collection   CAT 1

390a   **Here's a health to Queen Ann.** (Same music as No. **390**. New text to correspond to a new sovereign.)

MS   355
Printed collections   JOV 1 / PLE 1, 2, 4

391   **In drinking full bumpers.**   Three equal voices

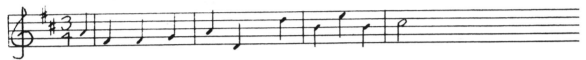

MSS   25, 158, 159, 169, 170, 355
Printed collections   CAT 1, 2, 3 / LAD 1, 2 / PLE 1, 2, 3, 4, 5 / SOC 1, 2

392   **Since my Phillis is fall'n.**   Three equal voices

MS   193
Printed collection   ESS 1
Remarks   This work appears in a collection of catches, canons and glees. The date, 1700, is under Clarke's name.

Ye cats that at midnight.   (Spurious: See No. **550**.)

393-399   Reserved for future entries.

INSTRUMENTAL MUSIC

Keyboard Suites

400   **Suite in G Major.**

   1   **Ground.**

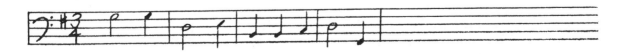

400–2 Almand.

3 Corant.

4 Aire.

5 Minuet.

MSS   Section 400.1 only: 30, 154

Printed collection   CHO 8

Remarks   A modern edition of the entire Suite may be found in J. A. Fuller-Maitland, *The Contemporaries of Purcell,* Vol. 5, Suite 1. A modern edition of the Minuet only may be found in K. Herrmann, *Contemporaries of Purcell,* p. 11.

401   Suite in A major.

1 Almand.

2 Round O.

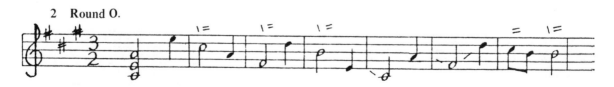

401–3 Jigg.

> *Printed collection* CHO 8
> *Remarks* A modern edition of the Suite may be found in J. A. Fuller-Maitland, *The Contemporaries of Purcell*, Vol. 5, Suite 2.

402 Suite in B minor.

1 Almand.

2 Corant.

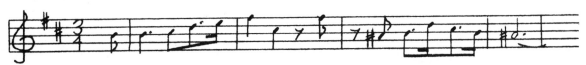

3 Saraband.

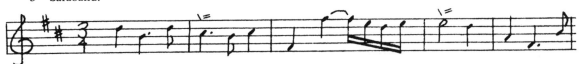

> *Printed collection* CHO 8
> *Remarks* A modern edition of the Suite may be found in J. A. Fuller-Maitland, *The Contemporaries of Purcell*, Vol. 5, Suite 3.

403 Suite in C minor.

1 Almand.

2 Corant.

403–3 **Minuet.**

MSS   Complete: 172 – Section 403.1: 30, 191 – Section 403.2: 30, 284
Printed collection   CHO 8
Remarks   *MS 30* (Cfm Mus. Ms. 653) substitutes a Jigg (anonymous) for the Minuet. A modern edition of the Suite may be found in J. A. Fuller-Maitland, *The Contemporaries of Purcell,* Vol. 5, Suite 4.

404   Suite in C major.

1   Almand.

2   Corant.

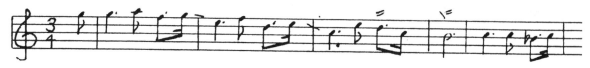

3   Jigg.

MSS   Sections 404.1 and 404.2: 30
Printed collection   CHO 8

405   Suite in C major.

1   An Entry.

2   Corant.

405–3 Minuet.

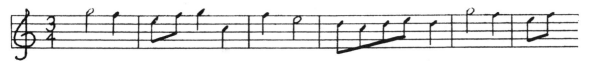

4 Donawert March.

Printed collection CHO 8

406 Suite in D major.

1 Almand.

2 Corant.

3 Minuet.

4 Duke of Marlbrough's March.

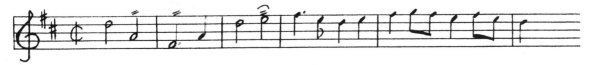

Printed collections Complete:CHO 8 / Section 406.4:COM 1
Remarks A modern edition of the Suite, except for the "Duke of Marlbrough's March," may be found in J. A. Fuller-Maitland, *The Contemporaries of Purcell*, Vol. 5, Suite 5.

407   Suite in A Minor.

1   Almand.

2   Corant.

3   Saraband

MS   171

408   Suite in G major.

1   Untitled dance movement.

2   Saraband.

3   Bory.

4   Minuet.

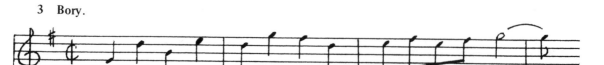

408–5 Untitled movement.

MS 171

409-419 Reserved for future entries.

Keyboard Grounds

---

420 Chaconne in C.

MSS 23, 30, 171
Remarks The incipit quoted here is according to *MS 171* (Lbm Add. 31465). The other sources differ slightly in their manner of breaking the chords.

421 A Ground in C.

MS 31
Printed collection NEW 1

A Ground. See No. **400.1**.

422 A Ground and Variations in F.

MS 31

423-429 Reserved for future entries.

Trumpet Tunes and Marches

Donawert March. See No. **405.4.**

430 The Duke of Gloucester's March. C major

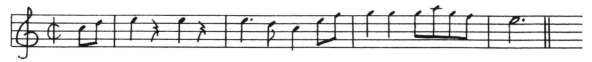

MS 156

Remarks The march is also in THE 1 (Theater musick . . . , 1698), p. 7, as a single melody possibly for violin; and in *MS 160* (Lbm Add. 30839) and *MSS 183-185* (Lbm Add. 39565-39567) in an arrangement for four instruments along with eight other pieces by Clarke, the collection called "Suite de Clark." See No. **497.1.**

The Duke of Marlbrough's March. See No. **406.4.**

431 The Emperor of Germany's March. D major

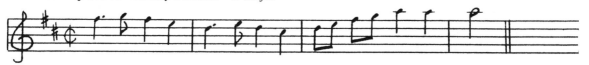

Printed collections CHO 1 / HAR 8

432 King William's March, Or The King's March. D major. Tune also used as the solo occasional song, "Whilst the French their arms discover." See No. **384.**

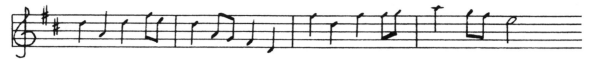

MS 156
Printed collections COM 1 / HAR 9 / SEL 1

433 A March. C major. Tune also used as the solo occasional song, "Drink, my boys, drink." See No. **380.** Also, as the solo occasional song, "Ulm is gon but basely won." See No. **383.**

MSS 156, 174
Printed collections CHO 1 / HAR 8

434 Mr. Shore's Trumpet Tune.   C major

MSS   156, 191, 327, 364

Printed collection   THE 1

Remarks   MS *327* (T 1508), in the hand of William Babel, is entitled "Scotch Tune Mr. Shors," in D major. This work is an arrangement for keyboard of the Scotch song, "Jockey was as brisk and Blithe a lad" (see No. **350**). In THE 1 (Theater Musick . . . , 1698), the tune only for violin, is called "Round O Mr. Clark Mr. Shor's Trumpet Tune." From this, the tune could be originally by Mr. Shore, but it is more probably by Clarke.

435 The Prince of Denmark's March.   D major

MSS   16, 171, 186, 191, 260, 327

Printed collections   CHO 1 / HAR 8 / SEL 4

Remarks   Formerly attributed to Henry Purcell. See Charles Cudworth, "Some New Facts about the Trumpet Voluntary," in: *Musical Times,* September 1953, pp. 401-403. Also see Charles Cudworth and Franklin Zimmerman, "The Trumpet Voluntary," in: *Music and Letters,* Vol. 41, no. 4, pp. 342-348, for other appearances of this popular tune. This article was reprinted in *Music–The AGO Magazine,* September 1969, pp. 28-30.

436 Prince Eugene's March.   D major

MSS   24, 50, 190, 191, 260, 279, 280

Printed collection   LAD 3

Remarks   Listed as No. S120 in Zimmerman's *Henry Purcell . . . Catalogue,* p. 349, where the author states, "actually was written by Jeremiah Clarke." The piece is not the same as "Prince Eugene's March into Italy," by John Shore (Ckc 110.22. Ref., No. **48**). The work was fitted with text and used by John Gay in his ballad opera, *Polly,* Act 3, London, 1729, p. 57. (Music and words, appendix, pp. 22-23) *MS 190* (Lbm Add. 52363 [1704]) calls the work "A March by Mr. Clarke."

Round O Mr. Clark.   See No. **434**.

437 Serenade.   D major

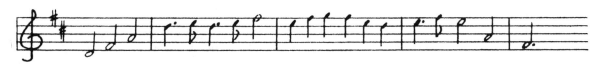

MSS   24, 156, 186, 189, 191, 282, 327

Printed collections   CHO 1 / HAR 8

Remarks   This tune appears in THE 1 (Theater Musick . . . , 1698) and APO 1 (Apollo's banquet . . . , 1701) for violin only. It was also arranged for four-part ensemble and called "Ecossais" in the "Suite de Clark" (see No. **497**). It was also used as the solo occasional song, "Twelve hundred years" (see No. **382**).

438   Trumpet Aire.   D major

MSS   279, where it is called "Trumpet Tune by Mr. Purcell"

        150, as the Second Act Tune for *The Island Princess* (see No. **300**)

Printed collection   THE 2

Remarks   This is the other famous trumpet tune. See Cudworth and Zimmerman, "The Trumpet Voluntary," in: *Music and Letters,* Vol. 41, October 1960, pp. 342-348, where the authors think the work is probably by Clarke, based on Eric Halfpenny's letter to the *Musical Times,* October 1960. Halfpenny bases his ascription of the tune to Clarke on the earliest printed source, THE 2 (Theater musick . . . the second book, 1699), where the work is called "Trumpet Aire by Mr. Clarke."

439   A Trumpet Minuett.   C major

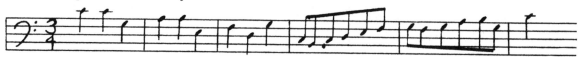

MSS   156, 191

Printed collections   CHO 1 / HAR 8

440-449   Reserved for future entries.

Miscellaneous Keyboard Pieces

450   Aire.   F minor

Printed collection   HAR 9

Remarks   The work was also arranged for four-part ensemble and included as number six in Clarke's airs in the comedy, *All for the Better* (see No. **310.6**).

451 An Aire Scotch.   F major

MS   156

452 Ayre.   C major

MS   282
Printed collections   CHO 1 / HAR 8
Remarks   Modern editions of this work may be found in Fuller-Maitland, *The Contemporaries of Purcell,* Vol. 5, p. 24; and Kurt Herrmann, *Contemporaries of Purcell,* p. 12.

453 Clark's Cibelle.

MSS   190, 279
Printed collection   APO 1
Remarks   There seem to be no printed sources of this work for harpsichord, but it is in APO 1 (Apollo's banquet . . . , 1701) for violin, and *MS 189* (Lbm Add. 47846) appears quite genuine, and contains other works by Clarke not so identified (see Nos. **435** and **457**). *MS 279* (Ob Ms.Mus.Sch. E.397) entitles the work, "Sybelle," while APO 1 calls it "Sebell." The three sources vary in ornamental and even melodic detail. The one quoted here is *MS 189*.

454 A Farewell.   F minor

Printed collection   HAR 9
Remarks   Also arranged for four-part ensemble and included as number 7 in Clarke's airs in the comedy, *All for the Better* (see No. **310.7**).

455 Gavotte.   F minor

Printed collection   HAR 9
Remarks   This work also comprises section 2 of the music from *All for the Better* (see No. **310.2**).

456 Hornpipe. F minor

Printed collection HAR 9

Remarks Also arranged for four-part ensemble and included as number 3 in Clarke's airs in the comedy *All for the Better* (see No. **310.3**).

457 King James's farewell. F major

MS 190
Printed collection LAD 3

458 Md.^m Subligny's Jigg. A major

Printed collection LAD 3

459 Minuet. F major

MS 30, 191
Printed collection LAD 3

460 Minuett (Trumpet Minuit). D major

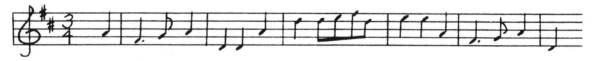

MS 30
Printed collection HAR 9
Remarks The MS version is in C major.

461 Minuett.   G minor

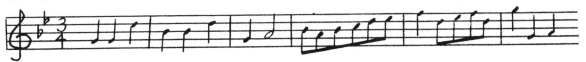

Printed collection   HAR 9
Remarks   This work should perhaps be placed in the doubtful category. There is no ascription in the source, and no other source is known to this writer which ascribes the work. This piece follows the Minuett, No. **460**, in the sources.

462 A new Cebell.   D major

MS   191
Printed collection   LAD 3
Remarks   This piece was also included in the *Division Flute II,* transposed into F major (see No. **484**).

463 A new Scotch tune.   E-flat major.

MS   191
Printed collection   LAD 3

464 Round O Minuett.   F major

Printed collection   HAR 9

465 Scotch air.   C major

MS   156
Remarks   No ascription is attached to the piece in the manuscript, but the index in the back lists Clarke as the composer. The style is consistent with the works known to be by him.

466   A Trip to Berry.   See No. **566.5.**

MS   30
Printed collection   LAD 3

467   A Trip to Case-horten.   D minor

Printed collections   HAR 9 / SEL 1
Remarks   SEL 1 (Select Lessons for the Violin) contains the tune only.

468-479   Reserved for future entries.

Pieces for Solo Violin or Recorder

480   Aire Mr Clark.   G minor

Printed collection   THE 2

481   Aire Mr. Clark.   G minor

Printed collection   THE 2

482   Ayre by Mr. Clark.   G minor, tune only

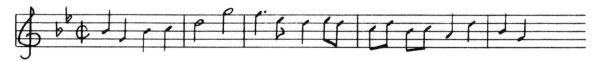

Printed collection   APO 1 / THE 2

The bonny grey-eyed morn. See No. **363**.

> *Printed collection* APO 1
> *Remarks* Violin with dance directions.

483 Case-horten.

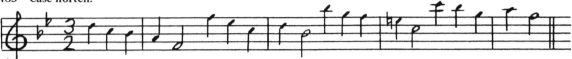

> *Printed collection* APO 1

484 Cibell in D (by Mr. Clark).

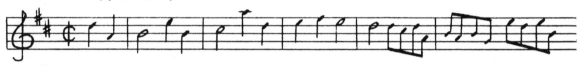

> *Printed collections* DIV 14, 15
> *Remarks* This piece appears transposed to F major in DIV 14 (the second part of the *Division Flute . . .*, 1707). The work was originally for harpsichord (see No. **462**).

485 Cibell in D (by Mr. Clark).

> *Printed collections* DIV 14, 15 / THE 2, 3

Come, Sweet Lass. See No. **336**.

> *MS* 280
> *Remarks* Transcribed for violin.

Could a Man be secure. See No. **337**.

> *Printed collection* SEL 4
> *Remarks* Transcribed for violin.

De'll Take the Wars. See No. **338**.

> *Printed collection* SEL 4
> *Remarks* Transcribed for violin with dance directions.

The Duke of Gloucester's March. See No. **430**.

> *Printed collection* THE 1
> *Remarks* Transcribed for violin.

486 Gavat.

Printed collection   APO 1

The Governor of Barbados' March.   See No. **406.4.**

Printed collection   COM 1
Remarks   Transcribed for violin from the Duke of Marlbrough's March.

487 Jigg Mr. Clark.   G minor

Printed collection   THE 2

The King's March.   See No. **432.**

Printed collection   SEL 1

March by Mr. J. Clark.   See No. **432.**

Printed collection   COM 1
Remarks   King William's March transposed to C for the violin.

488 Minuet on ye Duke of Gloster's birthday.

Printed collections   APO 1 / SEL 4
Remarks   This piece was used in the "Suite d'Clark" (see No. **497**).

489 Minuet in B-flat.

Printed collection   APO 1

490 Minuet by Mr. Clark in G minor.

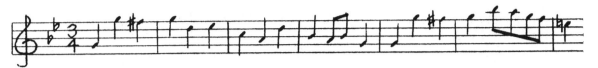

Printed collection   APO 1

491 Minuet Mr Clark.   G minor

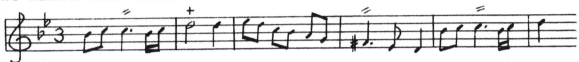

Printed collection   THE 2

Mr. Shore's Serenade by Mr. Clarke.   See No. **437.**

Printed collections   APO 1 / THE 1

492 Round O minuet Mr. Clark.   G minor

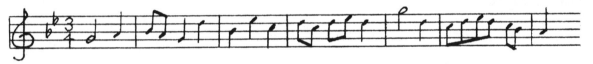

Printed collection   THE 1

493 Scotch Tune.   C major

Printed collections   APO 1 / SEL 4

494 Scotch Tune.   B-flat major

Printed collection   APO 1

Sebell Mr. Clark.   See No. **453.**

Printed collection   APO 1

Remarks   This work, originally for harpsichord, is also located in *MSS 190* and *279* (Lbm Add. 47846 and Ob.Ms.Mus.Sch. E.397).

MISCELLANEOUS COMPOSITIONS

495   **Canon.**   C major

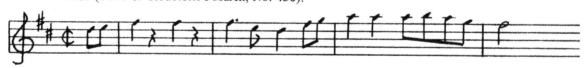

> *MS*   168
>
> *Remarks*   This work is either the beginning of an unfinished canon, or a complete short perpetual canon. The MS contains a collection of Purcell songs.

496   **Jig in g.**   2 vln, vla.   b

MUSIC NOT LOCATED

> *MS*   60

Lady Warton's faerwell.   See No. **311.2.**

497   **Suite de Clark.**   D major

    1   **Prelude** (Duke of Gloucester's March, No. **430**).

    2   **Minuet** (for violin alone in APO 1 [Apollo's banquet . . . , 1701], no. 40).   See No. **488.**

    3   **Cebel** (from Music on Henry Purcell's death, No. **200.5**).

497—4 **Rondeau** (Prince of Denmark's March, No. **435**).

5 **Ecossais** (Serenade, No. **437**).

6 **Bourrée.**

7 **Ecossais.**

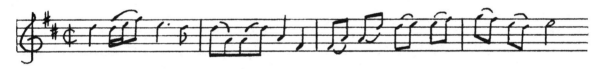

8 **Hornpipe.**

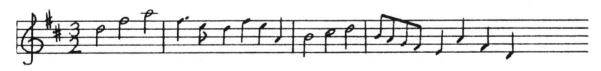

9 **Gigue.**

MSS 160, 183-185

Remarks *MS 160* (Lbm Add. 30839), fols. 55b-56v, is called "Suite for solo flute." It is actually the second treble part book of this suite. For incipits and discussion, see Charles Cudworth, "Some New Facts about the Trumpet Voluntary," in *Musical Times,* September 1953, pp. 401-403.

498-499 Reserved for future entries.

DOUBTFUL, SPURIOUS, OR UNLOCATED WORKS

Anthems

500 Behold God is my salvation. DOUBTFUL

MUSIC NOT LOCATED

> *MS* EX. Mus. 2/5, 9-10. ABB only. Second half eighteenth century
> *Remarks* No earlier sources located.

501 Hear my crying, O God. NOT LOCATED

MUSIC NOT LOCATED

> *Remarks* Listed in Myles B. Foster, *Anthems . . .* , p. 65, as being in Dr. A. H. Mann's "Unique Collection of Anthems, both in authograph and in print." Not traced.

502 I am the Resurrection. NOT LOCATED

MUSIC NOT LOCATED

> *Remarks* Listed in Myles B. Foster, *Anthems . . .* , p. 65, as being in Wells. Not traced.

503 O Jerusalem thou that killest. FULL/SATB. DOUBTFUL

MUSIC NOT LOCATED

> *MS* 7
> *Remarks* The music has not been seen by this writer. Letters of inquiry were sent in March and August 1970, with no answer.

504 Te Deum and Jubilate, Magnificat and Nunc Dimittis.   Organ.   SPURIOUS

> *MSS*   71a, 78a
> *Remarks*   This sacred polyphony has been wrongly ascribed to this Jer. Clarke in DRc. The work is actually by Dr. Clarke-Whitfeld.

505 Tell ye the daughters of Jerusalem.   Bc.   FULL /SATB.   DOUBTFUL

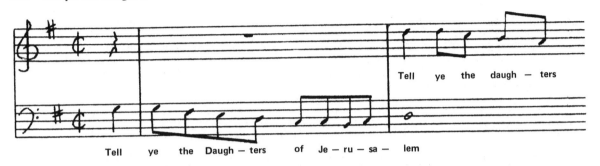

> *MS*   Lbm E.1492
> *Printed collection*   ROY 1
> *Remarks*   According to Williams, this anthem is by both Clarke and (Maurice) Green. Since there are no earlier sources, the authenticity is suspect.

506 Thou, O God art praised.   verse.   ab only.   DOUBTFUL, NOT LOCATED

MUSIC NOT LOCATED

> *MS*   208, 210?
> *Remarks*   The work was not located on inspection of these MSS, summer 1970.

507-519   Reserved for future entries.

Psalms and Hymns

520 Angel's Hymn.   DOUBTFUL

> *MS*   278
> *Remarks*   The source is late, with a woodwind prelude and interlude for clarinets and bassoon. No earlier sources, so the work is very doubtful.

521 Blest he whose heart with pity glows.   SPURIOUS

Blest   He,   whose   Heart   with   Pi — ty   glows,   Who

Printed collection   YOU 1

Remarks   The comment, "Set by the late Mr. Jeremiah Clarke" in the source is not correct. This hymn and No. **526** are two of the many versions of Tallis's Canon, which was originally composed for Matthew Parker's psalter (1566). A number of versions of this tune are described in Maurice Frost's English and *Scottish Psalm and Hymn Tunes 1543-1677*, (London, 1953), p. 391, and in Nicholas Temperley's article "The Adventures of a Hymn Tune" in *The Musical Times* 113 (April 1971), 375.

522 Canada. Hymn. ATTB. DOUBTFUL

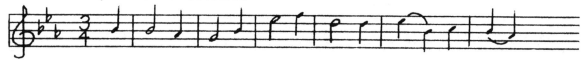

MS   278

523 Canterbury New.   Psalm 150, "O Praise the Lord." Hymn. TTB. DOUBTFUL

O   praise   the   Lord   in

MS   278

524 Cornhill. Pslam 51. DOUBTFUL

Make   me   to   hear   with   joy   thy   kind

MS   278

525 Cranbrook. Hymn tune. SATB. DOUBTFUL

MS   181

Remarks   MS 181 (Lbm Add. 36871) is from about 1800. Although the melody of Cranbrook has a trumpet tune quality, there is little else to suggest that it is by Clarke. No other early eighteenth-century music is contained in the volume.

526 Glory to thee, my God, this night. (For evening)   SPURIOUS

Glo — ry to Thee my   God this   Night; For   all the

Printed collection   YOU 1
Remarks   See remarks under No. **521.**

527 Nazarene (Christmas hymn by Clarke).   TTB.   DOUBTFUL

MS   278

528 Our God our Saviour is the Lord.   DOUBTFUL

Our   God   our   Sa — viour   is   the   Lord, For

Printed collection   YOU 1
Remarks   The only source located is one that is not trustworthy on versions of known psalms
(see No. **170**). Perhaps this work is by one of the other Jeremiah Clarkes.

529 Psalm 11.   TTB.   DOUBTFUL

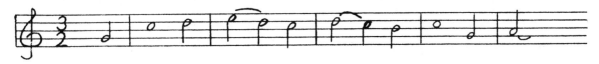

MS   278

530 Psalm 92.   (No text)   TTB.   DOUBTFUL

MS   278

531 St. Nicholas's. Psalm 44:23, 24, 26 or 18, 19, 20. DOUBTFUL

A — wake a — rise   let   seem — ing   sleep   no   long—er   thee   de — tain

MS   165

Printed collection   COL 6

Remarks   1790 is the earliest source; the work is perhaps by the Jer. Clarke (eighteenth century) of Birmingham.

532-539   Reserved for future entries.

Secular Vocal

540 The Sea Voyage. Music by H. and D. Purcell and Jer. Clarke.   NOT LOCATED

MUSIC NOT LOCATED

Remarks   An announcement in the *Daily Courant* states that this work was performed in Drury Lane at the Theatre Royal on May 26, 1710.

541 Twas within a furlong of Edinborough Town (Henry Purcell).   A Scotch song sung by the girl in *The Mock Marriage*.   Text by Thomas Scott, 1696.   G minor. **G, S**

Twas   with — in   a   fur — long   of   Ed — in — bor — ough

MS   156

Printed collections   COL 4 / SON 1 / WIT 1, 4, 10, 12 / *Deliciae Musicae* 3 (1696), 3-2 / facsimile in Cyrus Day, *The Songs of Thomas D'Urfey*, p. 108

Remarks   This song was used in the following stage productions:
1. *The Devil to Pay,* Or *The Wives metamorphos'd*. A play by Cha. Coffey.   Act 3. London, 1731, p. 49.
2. *Polly.* A ballad opera by Mr. Gay. Act 1. London, 1729, p. 7. Music on page 2 of the Appendix.
3. *The Chamber-maid.* A one-act ballad opera. Scene 3. London, 1730, p. 18.
4. *The Lover's Opera.* A ballad opera (no author indicated). London, 1730, p. 11.
5. The tune was used in Johnson's *Village Opera* (1729), fitted with a new text: "Now the bloom of spring."

For further information, see Claude Simpson, *The British Broadside Ballad*, pp. 635-636.

COL 1 (A Collection of new songs . . . , 1715) states "set by Mr. Henry Purcell."

542-549   Reserved for future entries.

Catches

550   **Ye cats that at midnight.**   SPURIOUS

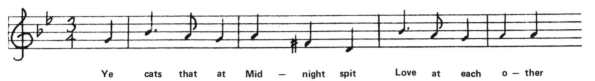

Ye   cats   that   at   Mid — night   spit   Love   at   each   o — ther

Printed collections   CAT 2, 3 / PLE 2

Remarks   The 1757 edition (CAT 3) of *The Catch Club* identifies the piece as "set by Mr. J. Clarke." The alphabetical table, however, gives it to Michael Wise, as does the earlier volume.

551-559   Reserved for future entries.

Instrumental

560   **The blessing of peace.**   DOUBTFUL

MS   17

Remarks   The late date of the manuscript, and the fact that there are no other pieces by Clarke or his contemporaries in it, cast considerable doubt on the authenticity of this piece. Although the style is quite consistent with that of Jeremiah Clarke (*ca.* 1673-1707), it perhaps is by the eighteenth-century Jeremiah Clarke of Birmingham, or J. Clarke-Whitfeld. The manuscript contains dance-step directions immediately after the piece.

561   **Cathedral Voluntaries.**   SPURIOUS

102   **How long wilt thou forget me.**

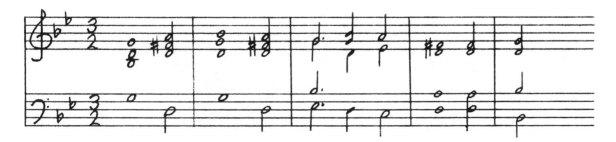

561–110 O Lord God of my Salvation.

MS 164

Remarks   The manuscript includes accompaniments to or voluntaries based on two anthems of Clarke. They are in the hand of, and presumably composed by, Vincent Novello, *ca.*1831. The anthems are "How long wilt thou forget me" (see No. **102**), and "O Lord God of my Salvation," (see No. **110**). Biographical notes on Clarke in the hand of Novello are included included in the margin.

562   Dorsetshire March.   SPURIOUS

MS 31

Remarks   Appears in *MS 31* (Cfm Mus. Ms. 668) after No. **421**, and so was thought to have been by Clarke. The MS contains works by later composers primarily.

563   Lessons for the Harpsichord or Spinet.   NOT LOCATED

Remarks   The April 22, 1704, edition of *Post Man* contains an advertisement for "J. Clarke's Lessons for the Harpsichord or Spinet," published by H. Playford in London, 1704.

564   A March.   C major.   DOUBTFUL

Printed collection   HAR 8

Remarks   This source does not attribute the March to any composer. No other indication exists that the work is by Clarke, except that it follows the March (No. **433**) and Ayre (No. **452**).

565   Mr. Clarkes tune.   DOUBTFUL

MS 48

566   Suite in F major.

1 Almand.   DOUBTFUL

2 Corant.   DOUBTFUL

3 Saraband.   DOUBTFUL

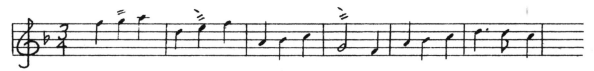

4 Minuet.   DOUBTFUL

5 A Trip to Berry.   See No. **466.**

MS   30

Remarks   "A Trip to Berry" is printed as a separate piece in LAD 3 (The Ladies Banquet . . . , 1704); it is the only part of the suite for which attribution to Clarke can be verified.

PLAYS CONTAINING MUSIC BY JEREMIAH CLARKE

Guide

This List of Plays is arranged alphabetically by title, each entry containing:
1. Title, author and publication information.
2. Production date and location, when available. Revivals in *italics*.
3. Music by Clarke.
4. Entry number of the works by Clarke in the Thematic Catalog.

All for the Better: Or, *The Infallible Cure,* by Francis Manning. London: printed and sold by B. Bragg, 1703.	1702, Drury Lane	Incidental music	**310**
The Amorous Miser: Or, *The Younger, the Wiser,* by Peter Anthony Motteux. London: Bragg, 1705.	1705	Song, Act 3	**368**
Anthony and Cleopatra, by Sir Charles Sedley. Printed as "Beauty the Conqueror: Or, The Death of Marc Antony" in: *The Miscellaneous Works of the Honourable Sir Charles Sedley.* London: J. Nutt, 1702.	February 1677. *1696*	Overture, instrumental music	**311**
The Bath: Or, *The Western Lass,* by Thomas D'Urfey. London: printed for Peter Buck, 1701.	May 1701, Drury Lane	Song, Act 5	**353**
The Campaigners: Or, *The Pleasant Adventures at Brussels,* by Thomas D'Urfey. London: printed for A. Baldwin, 1698.	*ca.* June 1698 Drury Lane	Song, Act 3	**349**

The Committee, by Sir Robert Howard. London: J. Tonson, 1722. 3rd ed.	1622. *October 1699, Drury Lane*	Song, not part of play	337
Cornish Comedy, by George Powell. London: printed for D. Brown, 1696.	*ca.* June 1696, Dorset Garden	Song, Act 2 Dialogue between Acts (MUSIC NOT EXTANT , dialogue printed in play) (EXTANT)	367 375 379
The Country Farmer, by Thomas D'Urfey. This is not a play, but is a song by Clarke on a text by D'Urfey.			342
Cynthia and Endymion: Or, *The Loves of the Dieties,* by Thomas D'Urfey. London: printed by W. Onley for Sam. Briscoe, in Russel-Street, Covenant-Garden; and R. Wellington at the Lute in St. Paul's Churchyard, 1697.	December 1696, Theatre Royal, Drury Lane		351
The Fond Husband: Or, *The Plotting Sisters,* by Thomas D'Urfey. London: printed by R. E. for R. Bentley and St. Magnes, 1685.	1676. *1697*	Song, not part of play	363
The History of Timon of Athens, the Man-Hater, by Thomas Shadwell. London: printed by J. M. for Henry Harringman, 1678.	January 1677-1678, Dorset Garden		333
The Island Princess: Or, *The Generous Portuguese,* by Peter Anthony Motteux. Adapted from the play by Fletcher. London: R. Wellington, 1699, 1701. Dublin: printed by S. Powell for G. Risk, 1726.	February 1699, Drury Lane	Overture and eleven instrumental pieces. The entertainment "The Four Seasons or Love in Every Age." Epilogue, "Now to you, ye dry wooers."	300.A 300.B 300.C
Love at First Sight, by David Crawford. London: printed for R. Basset, 1700.	March 1704, Lincoln's Inn Fields	Song, not in play. Text by T. D'Urfey.	364
Love's a Jest: Or, *The Comical Mistakes,* by Peter Anthony Motteux. London: printed for Peter Buck *et al,* 1696.	*ca.* June 1696, Lincoln's Inn Fields	Song, Act 1	359
Love's Last Shift: Or, *The Fool in Fashion,* by Colley Cibber. London: printed for H. Rhodes, R. Parker, and S. Briscoe, 1696.	January 1695-1696, Theatre Royal Drury Lane		365

Madame Fickle: Or, *The Witty False One,* by Thomas D'Urfey. London: printed for J. Magnus and R. Bentley, 1677.	1676. *1691*	Song, not part of play	**362**
The Mock Marriage, by Thomas Scott. London: printed for H. Rhodes, 1696.	*ca.* October 1695, Dorset Garden		**541**
The Relapse: Or, *Virtue in Danger,* by Sir John Vanbrugh. London: 1893.	November 1696, Drury Lane	Song, not part of play	**352**
Titus Andronicus: Or, *The Rape of Lavinia,* adapted by Edward Ravenscroft. London: printed by J. B. for J. Hindmarsh, 1687.	Drury Lane	Overture and act tune	**313**
The Virtuous Wife: Or, *Good Luck at Last,* by Thomas D'Urfey. London: printed in the Savoy by T. N. for R. Bentley and M. Magnus, 1680.	1679. *ca.1696-1697*	Nine act tunes	**314**
A Wife for any Man, by Thomas D'Urfey. NOT EXTANT. [See Cyrus L. Day, "A Lost Play by D'Urfey," *Modern Language Notes* 49 (1934), 332-334.]	*ca.* 1695-1697	Nine act tunes	**315**
The World in the Moon, by Elkanah Settle. London: printed for Abel Roper, 1697.	June 1697, Dorset Garden	Prologue. The entertainment "Within this happy World Above."	**301.A** **301.B** **369**
		Song, not part of play.	**347**

BIBLIOGRAPHY

Note

The following list makes no attempt at being exhaustive, but is limited to works referred to in the catalog, and other works used in the compilation. For a more complete bibliography of the period, the reader should consult Franklin Zimmerman's *Henry Purcell, 1659-1695, His Life and Times.*

ARBER, Edward, ed. *The Term Catalogues, 1668-1709 A.D.;* with a Number for Easter Term, 1711 A.D. London: privately printed, 1903-1906.
A contemporary bibliography of English literature in the reigns of Charles II, James II, William & Mary, and Anne.

BARCLAY-SQUIRE, W. *Catalogue of Printed Music Published Between 1487 and 1800 Now in the British Museum.* London: British Museum, 1912.

————. "Jeremiah Clarke" in: Leslie STEPHEN, ed, *Dictionary of National Biography* 5 (London: Smith, Elder & Co., 1887), 430-431.

BUMPUS, John S. *A History of English Cathedral Music, 1549-1889.* 2 vols. London: Laurie, (1908).

BURNEY, Charles. *A General History of Music from the Earliest Ages to the Present Period (1789) by Charles Burney . . . with Critical and Historical Notes by Frank Mercer.* 2 vols. New York: Harcourt, Brace and Company, (1935).

CUDWORTH, Charles. "Jeremiah Clarke" in: Friedrich BLUME, ed, *Die Musik in Geschichte und Gegenwart, Allgemeine Enzyklopädie der Musik* 2 (Kassel: Bärenreiter, 1952), 1462-1464.

————. "Some New Facts about the Trumpet Voluntary," *Musical Times* 94 (September 1953), 401-403.

CUDWORTH, Charles, and Franklin ZIMMERMAN. "The Trumpet Voluntary," *Music and Letters* 41/no. 4 (October 1960), 342-348. Reprinted in *Music–The AGO Magazine* 3/no. 9 (September 1969), 28-30.

Bibliography

DANIEL, Ralph T. *The Anthem in New England Before 1800.* Evanston: Northwestern University Press, 1966.

DART, Thurston. "The Cibell," *Revue Belge de Musicologie* 6/no. 1 (1952), 24-30.

DAVEY, Henry. *History of English Music.* 2nd ed. London: J. Curwen & Sons, 1921.

DAY, Cyrus Lawrence. *The Songs of Thomas D'Urfey.* Cambridge, Mass.: Harvard University Press, 1933.

DAY, Cyrus Lawrence and E. B. MURRIE. *English Song Books, 1651-1707.* London: 1940.

deLAFONTAINE, Henry Cart, ed. *The King's Musick. A Transcript of Records Relating to Music and Musicians (1460-1700).* London: Novello & Co., (1909).

DENT, Edward J. *Foundations of English Opera.* Cambridge, Mass.: Cambridge University Press, 1928.

EITNER, Robert. *Quellen-Lexikon der Musiker und Musikgelehrten der Christlichen Zeitrechnung bis zur Mitte des neunzehnten Jahrhunderts.* New York: Musurgia, *ca.* 1898.

EVELYN, John. *Diary.* Edited by Austin Dobson. 3 vols. London: Macmillan and Co., Ltd., 1906.

FELLOWES, Edmund H. *Organists and Masters of the Choirsters of St. George's Chapel in Windsor Castle.* London: Society for the Promotion of Christian Knowledge, 1940.

———. *English Cathedral Music.* Revised by J. A. Westrup. London: Methuen & Co., 1969.

FISKE, Roger. *English Theatre Music in the Eighteenth Century.* London: Oxford University Press, 1973.

FOSTER, Myles B. *Anthems and Anthem Composers. An Essay Upon the Development of the Anthem from the Time of the Reformation to the End of the Nineteenth Century* (London: Novello & Co., Ltd., 1901), pp. 59, 65.

FULLER-MAITLAND, J. A., and A. H. MANN. *Catalogue of the Music in the Fitzwilliam Museum, Cambridge.* London: C. J. Clay, 1893.

FULLER-MAITLAND, J. A., ed. *The Contemporaries of Purcell.* London: J. & W. Chester, 1921.

GUSTAFSON, Bruce. *The Sources of Seventeenth-Century French Harpsichord Music.* Dissertation, University of Michigan, 1976.

HARLEY, John. "Music and Musicians in Restoration London," *Musical Quarterly* 40 (October 1954), 509-520.

———. *Music in Purcell's London.* London: Dennis Dobson, 1968.

HAUN, Eugene. *But Hark! More Harmony. The Libretti of Restoration Opera in English.* Ypsilanti: Eastern Michigan University, 1971.

HAWKINS, Sir John. *A General History of the Science and Practice of Music.* London: J. Alfred Novello, 1853.

HAYES, Philip. Short account of Jeremiah Clark in the hand of Dr. Philip Hayes. Lbm Add. 33235, fol. 2. London: British Museum, late eighteenth century.

HERRMANN, Kurt, ed. *Contemporaries of Purcell.* London: Hinrichsen edition, (193-?).

HUGHES-HUGHES, Augustus. *Catalogue of Manuscript Music in the British Museum.* London: British Museum, 1906.

    Vol. 1   Sacred Vocal Music
    Vol. 2   Secular Vocal Music
    Vol. 3   Instrumental Music, Treatises, etc.

The Hymnal of the Protestant Episcopal Church in the United States of America, 1940. New York: The Church Pension Fund, 1943.

HUSK, William H. *An Account of the Musical Celebrations on St. Cecilia's Day in the Sixteenth, Seventeenth and Eighteenth Centuries.* London: 1857.

LIGHTWOOD, James T. *Hymn-Tunes and Their Story.* London: C. H. Kelly, (1905).

McAFFEE, Helen. *Pepys on the Restoration Stage.* New Haven: Yale University Press, 1916.

McGUINNESS, Rosamond. "The Chronology of John Blow's Court Odes," *Music and Letters* 44/no. 2 (April 1965), 102-121.

MELLERS, Wilfred. *Harmonious Meeting. A Study of the Relationship between English Music, Poetry and Theatre, c.1600-1900.* London: Dennis Dobson, 1965.

MOORE, Robert Etheridge. *Henry Purcell and the Restoration Theatre.* Cambridge, Mass.: Harvard University Press, 1961.

NICOLL, Allardyce. *A History of English Drama 1660-1900.* Cambridge, Mass.: Cambridge University Press, 1952-1959.

    Vol. 1   *Restoration Drama 1600-1700.* 4th ed.
    Vol. 2   *Early Eighteenth Century Drama.* 3rd ed.
    Vol. 6   *A Short-Title Alphabetical Catalogue of Plays Produced or Printed in England from 1660-1900.*

NORTH, Roger. *Memoirs of Musick.* Edited by Edward F. Rimbault. London: George Bell, 1846. Original North Book, 1728.

Post Boy, Post Man. See Michael TILMOUTH, *A Calendar of References to Music in Newspapers Published in London and the Provinces (1660-1719).*

PULVER, Jeffrey. *A Biographical Dictionary of Old English Music.* London: Kegan Paul, Trench, Trubner & Co., Ltd., 1927.

RIMBAULT, Edward F. *Cathedral Services.* London: J. A. Novello, 1847.

SCHNAPPER, Edith, ed. *The British Union-Catalogue of Early Music Printed Before the Year 1801. A Record of the Holdings of Over One Hundred Libraries Throughout the British Isles.* London: Butterworth's Scientific Publications, 1957.

SHAW, Harold Watkins. "Jeremiah Clarke" and "John Blow" in: Eric BLOM, ed, *Grove's Dictionary of Music and Musicians.* 5th ed. New York: St. Martin's Press, Inc., 1954. Vol. 1, pp. 768-775; Vol. 2, pp. 331-333.

Bibliography

SIMPSON, Claude. *The British-Broadside Ballad and Its Music.* New Brunswick: Rutgers University Press, 1966.

SMITH, William C. *A Bibliography of the Musical Works Published by John Walsh During the Years 1695-1720.* London: Oxford University Press, 1948.

TAYLOR, Thomas F. "Jeremiah Clarke's Music for Harpsichord," *The Diapason* (September 1969), pp. 24-25.

————. "Jeremiah Clarke's Trumpet Tunes: Another View of Origins," *Musical Quarterly* 56/no. 3 (July 1970), 455-463.

THORP, Willard, ed. *Songs from the Restoration Theater.* Princeton: Princeton University Press, 1934.

TILMOUTH, Michael. *A Calendar of References to Music in Newspapers Published in London and the Provinces (1660-1719).* Research chronicle, no. 1, 1961. London: Royal Musical Association.

WALKER, Ernest. *A History of Music in England.* Revised and enlarged by J. A. Westrup. 3rd. ed. Oxford: Clarendon Press, 1952.

WEST, John E. *Cathedral Organists Past and Present. A Record of the Succession of Organists of the Cathedrals, Chapels Royal, and Principal Collegiate Churches of the United Kingdom, from About the Period of the Reformation until the Present Day.* London: Novello & Co., Ltd., 1899.

WESTRUP, Jack A. *Purcell.* London: J. M. Dent and Sons, Ltd., 1947. New York: Collier Books, 1962.

WILLIAMS, Ralph Vaughan, ed. *The English Hymnal with Tunes.* London: H. Milford, 1924.

WING, Donald. *Short-title Catalogue of Books Printed in England, Scotland, Ireland, Wales and British America and of Other English Books Printed in Other Countries 1641-1700.* New York: Columbia University Press, 1945-1951.

ZIMMERMAN, Franklin B. *Henry Purcell 1659-1695, An Analytical Catalogue of His Music.* New York: St. Martin's Press, 1963.

————. *Henry Purcell 1659-1695, His Life and Times.* New York: St. Martin's Press, 1967.

INDEX OF MANUSCRIPTS

Guide

With the exception of the Gostling manuscript in the University of Texas Library, all the important early manuscript sources of Clarke's compositions are contained in British libraries. Shortly before research for the present study was undertaken, the British collections were surveyed by Mr. Richard Andrewes of Cambridge University, for the *International Inventory of Musical Sources* (RISM). The unpublished results of Mr. Andrewes' work were made available to the author through the gracious generosity of Mssrs. Christopher Powell and Charles Cudworth of Cambridge and A. Hyatt King of London during the summer of 1970.

With this preview, the task of inspecting manuscript sources was lightened considerably. Each source was located and the library number, foliation or pagination, and positive identification of the works verified. Many of the manuscript datings included herein were made by Mr. Andrewes, although most dates were checked when the manuscripts were inspected in 1970.

This Index of Manuscripts is arranged alphabetically by library sigla and then by the library catalog number. Each entry contains:

1. Manuscript number.
2. Library catalog number.
3. Date or other description.
4. Foliation or pagination in the source given, when available.
5. Entry number of the works by Clarke in the Thematic Catalog.

EIRE / IRELAND

Dcc: Christ Church Cathedral, Dublin

1	Old Loft Books 2-4	3 parts / ATB / first half 18th century		**106, 115**
2	Old Loft Books 6-7	2 parts / AB / *ca.* 1780		**117**
3	Old Loft Book 7	B, bc / second quarter 18th century		**105**
4	Organ Book 8	organ / late 18th century		**105, 117**
5	Organ Book 13	organ / fourth quarter 18th century		**110**
6	Score Book 8	score / mid 18th century	pp. 49-59	**105**
7	Score Book 14	score / *ca.* 1765	pp. 44-48	**113**
			pp. 41-44	**503**
8	Score Book 16	score / 1769 and mid 18th century	pp. 141-151	**110**
			pp. 184-196	**117**

EIRE / IRELAND

Dpc: St. Patrick's Cathedral, Dublin

9	C.3 1, 3	2 parts / TA / first half 18th century		**105**
10	C.3. 1, 4, 6	3 parts / ABA / first half 18th century		**106**
11	C.3. 1, 4-6	4 parts / ABAB / second half 18th century		**110**
12	C.3. 2-3, 5	3 parts / TTB / first half 18th century		**106, 110**
13	C.3 2, 4-6	4 parts / ABTB / first half 18th century		**105**

Dtc: Trinity College, Dublin

14	I.6.44	organ / fourth quarter 18th century		**102**
15	I.6.47	organ / first half 18th century		**105**

GREAT BRITAIN

AY: Bucks County Record Office, Aylesbury

16	D/DR/10/6a	keyboard / first half 18th century	fols. 13v-14v	**435**

Bp: Public Library, Birmingham

17	167208	keyboard / after 1794	p. 91	**560**

Bu: University Library, Birmingham

18	Ms. 5003	score / *ca.*1720	fols. 57-63	**105**

CA: Cathedral Libraries, Canterbury

[Nos. 19-21: a set of part books, incomplete]

19	Alto	A / 18th century		**105, 110, 117**
20	Bass	B / 18th century		**102, 110, 113**
21	Tenor	T / 18th century (2 copies)		**105, 110** **113, 117**

CDp: Public Library, Cardiff

22	M.C.1. 38	voice / bc / inscribed "James Lovett his Book April 27, 1701"	pp. 175-182	**300.B.5 (376)**
			pp. 37-39	**335**
			p. 1	**347**
			pp. 161-163	**352**
			pp. 132-134	**366**
			pp. 98-100	**380**
23	M.C.1. 39 (J)	keyboard / early 18th century	fols. 51v-54	**420**
24	M.C.1. 39 (K)	keyboard / *ca.* 1704-1705	fol. 34v	**436**
			fol. 35	**437**

Cfm: Fitzwilliam Museum, Cambridge

25	Mus. Ms. 120 (30 G 24)	S / *ca.*1732	p. 321	**391**
26	Mus. Ms. 152 (32 F 23)	organ / *ca.*1705 (perhaps in the hand of John Blow) / fol. 15v, incomplete: first 2 verses only / fol. 20, final 45 measures / fol. 12, end only	fol. 15v fol. 12 fol. 20	**106** **115** **119**

27	Mus. Ms. 238 (52 D 20)	score / 18th century	fols. 33-35	**113**
28	Mus. Ms. 239 (52 D 21)	score / 18th century (in the hand of Thomas Barrow)	pp. 163-172	**117**
			pp. 179-181	**150**
29	Mus. Ms. 276 (52 A 17)	score / *ca.* 1775 (in the hand of William Cole)	pp. 9-15	**105**
			pp. 162-173	**107**
			pp. 258-263	**113**
			pp. 123-139	**117**
30	Mus. Ms. 653 (52 B 7)	keyboard / first half 18th century	pp. 110-111	**400.1**
			p. 37	**403.1**
			p. 38	**403.2**
			p. 6	**404.1 & 2**
			pp. 4-5	**420**
			p. 41	**459**
			p. 20	**460**
			p. 49	**466**
			pp. 47-49	**566**
31	Mus. Ms. 668 (52 C 11)	keyboard / second half 18th century / fols. 73r-73v, misbound	fols. 75v, 73r-73v	**421**
			fols. 52v-54	**422**
			fol. 73v	**562**
32	Mus. Ms. 669 (52 C 12)	organ / first quarter 18th century	pp. 32-33	**102**

Cjc: St. John's College, Cambridge

33	Chapel Ms. O. 11	score / 18th century	pp. 108-112	**113**
			pp. 130-140	**117**
			pp. 141-150	**119**
34	Chapel Ms. O.14	organ / first half 18th century		**106, 113**
35	Chapel Ms. Q.1/1-8	8 parts		**119**

[Nos. 36-44: a set of part books]

36	Chapel Ms. T.1	S / second half 18th century		**105?, 113, 117**
37	Chapel Ms. T.2	A / 18th century		**105?, 113, 117**
38	Chapel Ms. T.3	T / second half 18th century		**105?, 117**
39	Chapel Ms. T.4	B / first quarter 18th century		**105?, 113**
40	Chapel Ms. T.5	S / 18th century		**105?, 113, 117**
41	Chapel Ms. T.6	A / 18th century		**105?, 113, 117**
42	Chapel Ms. T.7	T / first half 18th century		**105?, 113, 117**
43	Chapel Ms. T.8	B / first half 18th century		**113, 117**
44	Chapel Ms. T.9	B / mid 18th century		**105?, 113**
45	Chapel Ms. box of fragments	organ / 18th century		**113, 115**

Ckc: King's College, Cambridge

46	Ms. 9	organ / first half 18th century	fols. 73v-74	**113**
			fol. 137, no. 24	**153**
47	Ms. 21	score / 18th century	fols. 83v-86	**110**
			fols. 67v-68v	**113**
48	Ms. 185	melody only / second half seventeenth century		**565**
49	Ms. 268	4 parts / SATB / *ca.* 1739		**160**
50	Ms. 330	flute / 18th century / fol. 12v, melody only	fol. 12v	**436**

GREAT BRITAIN

Ckc: King's College, Cambridge

GREAT BRITAIN

DRc: Cathedral Library, Durham

93	Ms. Mus. C.19	B / first quarter 18th century	p. 476	**102**
			pp. 321-323	**104**
			pp. 320-321	**105**
			pp. 334-336	**110**
			pp. 324-326	**113**
			p. 327	**117**
94	Ms. Mus. C.19a	T / *ca.* 1715	pp. 119-121	**110**
95	Ms. Mus. C.21	T / first quarter 18th century	p. 180	**102**
			pp. 107-110	**110**
96	Ms. Mus. C.27	B / *ca.* 1700-1710	pp. 371-373	**101**
			pp. 353-358	**105**
			pp. 92-93	**113**
			pp. 374-377	**115**
			pp. 255-260	**116**
			pp. 346-349	**117**
97	Ms. Mus. C.28	B / *ca.* 1700-1710	pp. 436-437	**105**
			pp. 153-156	**110**
			pp. 456-458	**113**
			pp. 201-204	**116**
98	Ms. Mus. C.29	B / after 1717	pp. 173-174v	**102**
			pp. 108-111v	**110**
99	Ms. Mus. C.34	B / mid 18th century	pp. 155-158	**116**
100	Ms. Mus. C.35	T / after 1717	p. 175	**102**
			pp. 88-91v	**110**
101	Ms. Mus. M.90	score, late 18th century–early 19th century	fols. 14v-15	**160**
102	Ms. Mus. M.174	score / second half 18th century	fols. 5v-6	**114**
			fols. 8v-9	**140**
			fols. 6v-7	**160**

EL: Cathedral Library, Ely

103	No. 2	organ / first quarter 18th century		**105?, 113**
104	No. 8	score / mid 18th century	pp. 172-176	**113**
105	No. 9	organ / mid 18th century		**102**
		score / first quarter 18th century	pp. 135-138	**104**
			pp. 269-273	**105**
106	No. 15	score / first quarter 18th century	pp. 73-82	**105**
107	No. 16	score / first quarter 18th century	pp. 162-168	**105**
108	No. 19	score / first quarter 18th century	pp. 25-36	**117**
108a	No. 20	score / first quarter 18th century	pp. 7-17	**107**
109	No. 25	B / first quarter 18th century		**105?, 113**
110	No. 26	T / first quarter 18th century		**102, 105?, 113**
111	No. 27	B / second half 18th century		**105?**
112	No. 28	T / mid 18th century		**102**
113	No. 29	B / second quarter 18th century		**102, 105?, 113**
114	No. 30	A / mid 18th century		**102, 105?, 113**
115	No. 31	2 parts / TB / second half 18th century		**102, 105?, 113**
116	No. 32	score / second half 18th century		**105**
117	No. 33	2 parts / TB / first half 18th century		**105?**
118	No. 34	2 parts / SB / second half 18th century		**102, 105?, 113**

GREAT BRITAIN

Lbm: British Museum, London

152	Add. 17840	score / first quarter 18th century	fols. 152-154v	**105**
153	Add. 17842	score / 18th century	fols. 94v-100v	**105**
154	Add. 17853	score / fourth quarter 18th century	fols. 47v-48v	**400.1**
155	Add. 19759	S / 17th century—first quarter 18th century	fol. 45v	**342**
156	Add. 22099	keyboard / *ca.* 1704-1707	fol. 55	**160**
			fol. 90	**170**
			fol. 6v	**336**
			fol. 5	**342**
			fol. 4v	**350**
			fol. 7	**363**
			fol. 4v	**430**
			fols. 7-7v	**432**
			fol. 5v	**433**
			fol. 4v	**434**
			fol. 6v	**437**
			fol. 6	**439**
			fol. 6v	**451**
			fol. 5v	**465**
			fol. 9	**541**
157	Add. 29371	S / 18th century / fol. 50, tune only	fol. 42v	**336**
			fol. 50	**338**
158	Add. 29386	score / *ca.* 1762	fol. 18v	**390**
			fol. 19	**391**
159	Add. 30273	3-part canon / *ca.* 1833	fol. 44	**391**
160	Add. 30839	alto recorder / late 17th century—early 18th century (part of a 4 book set, see Add. 39565-39567)	fols. 55v-56v	**497**
161	Add. 30931	score / late 17th century—early 18th century	fols. 121v-124v	**105**
162	Add. 30932	score / late 17th century—early 18th century	fols. 66-67v	**113**
			fols. 113-117v	**117**
163	Add. 30934	score / *ca.* 1695	fols. 3-34v	**200**
164	Add. 31120	organ score / *ca.* 1831 (organ parts by Vincent Novello)	fol. 5	**102**
			fol. 6	**110**
			fols. 5-6	**561**
165	Add. 31420	S / bc	fol. 54	**164**
			fol. 19	**165**
			fol. 16v	**169**
			fol. 18v	**170**
			fol. 17	**531**
166	Add. 31452	score / 18th century	fols. 82v-100	**204.1-204.9**
167	Add. 31453	score / first quarter 18th century	fol. 169	**336**
			fol. 178v	**344**
			fol. 177v	**350**
			fol. 169	**370**
168	Add. 31461	S / first quarter 18th century	fol. 5v	**495**
169	Add. 31462	3-part canon / fourth quarter 18th century		**390, 391**

170	Add. 31463	3-part canon / fourth quarter 18th century	fol. 15v	**390**
			fol. 37v	**391**
171	Add. 31465	keyboard / first quarter 18th century	fols. 48v-50v	**407**
			fols. 51-53	**408**
			fols. 55v-57v	**420**
			fols. 16v-17	**435**
172	Add. 31467	keyboard / 1735	fols. 70v-71	**403**
173	Add. 31812	score / 1828 (copied by R.J.S. Stevens)	fols. 1-31	**200**
			fols. 32-42	**203**
174	Add. 31813	score / fourth quarter 18th century	fols. 84-98v	**206**
			fols. 99-106v	**301.A**
			fols. 107-121	**301.B**
			fol. 130v	**301.B.3 (339)**
			fol. 127v	**342**
			fol. 131v	**344**
			fol. 131	**347**
			fol. 127	**353**
			fol. 104v	**361**
			fol. 129	**363**
			fol. 132	**364**
			fol. 129v	**367**
			fol. 130	**368**
			fol. 128	**384**
			fol. 128v	**433**
175	Add. 31819	organ / fourth quarter 18th century	fol. 68	**165**
176	Add. 31821	score with Bc / 1828 / R. Stevens	fols. 55v-59v	**101**
			fols. 68v-75	**106**
			fols. 60v-65v	**109**
			fols. 49v-54	**117**
			fols. 66-67v	**142**
177	Add. 33351	S / 18th century	fol. 16v	**368**
178	Add. 33568	score / *ca.*1768	fols. 9-11	**100**
179	Add. 34204	recorder / *ca.*1708	fol. 3	**363**
180	Add. 35043	1 instrumental part / *ca.*1697	fols. 92-93v	**312**
			fols. 38-39	**314**
			fols. 71-72	**315**
181	Add. 36871	score / *ca.*1800	fols. 5v-6	**525**
182	Add. 37072	score / after 1720	fols. 65v-69	**105**

[Nos. 183-185: a set of part books, with Add. 38039]

183	Add. 39565	soprano recorder / late 17th century– early 18th century	fols. 55-57v	**497**
184	Add. 39566	tenor recorder / late 17th century– early 18th century	fols. 55-57v	**497**
185	Add. 39567	bass recorder / late 17th century– early 18th century	fols. 55-57v	**497**
186	Add. 39569	keyboard / 1702 (in hand of William Babel) / no. **435**, item 100 / no. **437**, item 99	p. 72	**435**
			p. 72	**437**
187	Add. 39572	score / 1768	fols. 95v-98v	**110**
188	Add. 39868	organ / 1724 (organ book of John Bennet)	fols. 5v-7	**113**
189	Add. 47446	1 instrumental part / 1722 / rhythm and meter altered	p. 71	**437**

GREAT BRITAIN

Lbm: British Museum, London

209	Ms. Mus. 15	T / 1709-1710		**101, 102, 105?** **113, 117, 120**
210	Ms. Mus. 16	B / 1709-1710		**101, 102, 105?** **113, 117, 120**
211	Ms. Mus. 17	A / 1710-1711		**101, 113**
212	Ms. Mus. 18	B / 1709-1711		**101, 105?, 113,** **117, 120**
213	Ms. Mus. 19	A / 18th century		**105?, 113,** **117, 120**
214	Ms. Mus. 20	T / first half 18th century		**101, 105?,** **113, 117, 120**
215	Ms. Mus. 21	2 parts / TB / first half 18th century		**101, 105?,** **113, 117, 120**
216	Ms. Mus. 22	3 parts / TBB / first half 18th century		**101, 105?,** **113, 117, 120**
217	Ms. Mus. 24	B (with A or T for some pieces) / first quarter 18th century		**101, 105?,** **113, 117, 120**
218	Ms. Mus. 25	T or B / 18th century		**102, 105?, 110,** **113, 117, 120**
219	Ms. Mus. 26	B / first half 18th century		**105?, 113,** **117, 120**
220	Ms. Mus. 27	A / first half 18th century		**117**
221	Ms. Mus. 28	B / first half 18th century		**105?, 117**
222	Ms. Mus. 29	A / *ca.* 1780		**102, 110**
223	Ms. Mus. 30	T / *ca.* 1780		**102, 110**
224	Ms. Mus. 31	B / *ca.* 1780		**102, 110**
225	Ms. Mus. 32	A / *ca.* 1780		**105?, 110**
226	Ms. Mus. 33	T / *ca.* 1780		**102, 110**
227	Ms. Mus. 34	B / *ca.* 1780		**102, 110**
228	Ms. Mus. 60	organ / fourth quarter 18th century		**110, 113**
229	Ms. Mus. 64	organ / fourth quarter 18th century		**102**

LI: Cathedral Library, Lincoln

230	Kk.1.6a	organ / August 29, 1754, exam[ined] by me Wm. Pawson		**113**
231	Organ Book 2	organ / *ca.* 1760		**102, 105?, 117**
232	Set A	2 parts / TB / 1713		**113**
233	Set B	4 parts / TBAB / *ca.* 1701-1711		**101, 102,** **105?, 116**
234	Set C	T / *ca.* 1705		**105?**
235	Set D	B / *ca.* 1720		**105?**
236	Set E	B / second half 18th century		**113**

Lsp: St. Paul's Cathedral, London

237	Organ Vol. 1	organ / *ca.* 1719	pp. 42-50	**105**
238	Organ Vol. 3	organ / 18th century	pp. 82-87	**110**
			pp. 100-103	**113**
239	Organ Vol. 5	organ / fourth quarter 18th century	pp. 420-422	**105**
			pp. 561-563	**110**
			pp. 409-411	**117**
240	Organ Vol. 6	organ / fourth quarter 18th century	p. 786	**102**
			pp. 850-852	**105**

GREAT BRITAIN

Lsp: St. Paul's Cathedral, London

241	Ms. Alto 3	A / first quarter 18th century	p. 112	**101**
			p. 112	**102**
			pp. 110-111	**105**
			pp. 16-17	**113**
			pp. 109-110	**117**
			pp. 121-122	**120**
242	Ms. Tenor 4	T / first quarter 18th century	pp. 62-64	**101**
			p. 64	**102**
			pp. 57-59	**105**
			pp. 15-16	**113**
			pp. 54-55	**117**
			pp. 60-62	**120**
243	Ms. Bass 3	B / first quarter 18th century	p. 138	**101**
			p. 137	**102**
			p. 135	**105**
			pp. 14-15	**113**
			pp. 134-135	**117**
			p. 136	**120**
244	Ms. Alto 4	A / 1766 / score on added leaf, recto, p. 32b	pp. 32b-v	**150**
245	Ms. Alto 5	A / third quarter 18th century	p. 116	**102**
			pp. 36-38v	**110**
246	Ms. Alto 6	A / second half 18th century	pp. 39-43	**117**
247	Ms. Alto 7	A / second half 18th century	p. 34	**117**
248	Ms. Bass 4	B / third quarter 18th century	pp. 40-45	**105**
			pp. 21-23v	**110**
			pp. 50-51v	**113**
249	Ms. Bass 5	B / third quarter 18th century	pp. 39-41	**110**
			pp. 64-66	**113**
250	Ms. Bass 8	B / second half 18th century	pp. 42-43	**117**
251	Ms. Bass 9	B / second half 18th century	pp. 91-95	**117**
252	Ms. Tenor 2	T / 1766		**117**
253	Ms. Tenor 5	T / second half 18th century	p. 68	**117**
254	Ms. Tenor 6	T / second half 18th century	pp. 65-69	**117**
255	Ms. Tenor 7	T / third quarter 18th century	pp. 77-78v	**102**
			pp. 104-108v	**105**
			pp. 31-33	**110**
			pp. 58-60	**113**
256	Ms. Treble 3	S / 1766		**102, 117, 150**
257	Ms. Treble 4	S / 1766		**117, 150**
258	Ms. Treble 6	S / first quarter 18th century		**110**

Mp: Public Libraries, Manchester

259	BRm 370 Cp21	organ / May 1707		**118**

NH: Record Office, Northampton

260	M (TM) 657	soprano recorder / 18th century / no. **435**, in f / no. **436**, melody only in f		**435, 436**

Ob: Bodleian Library, Oxford

261	Ms. Mus. c.6	score / first quarter 18th century	fols. 2-22	**206**
262	Ms. Mus. c.41	B / second half 18th century	fol. 40	**113**
263	Ms. Mus. c.50	S / *ca.*1750–second half of 18th century / with set *MSS 268-277,* ms. in various hands	pp. 87-88 pp. 86-87	**102** **117**
264	Ms. Mus. c.58	score / first quarter 18th century	fols. 25-31 fols. 43-47v	**106** **115**
265	Ms. Mus. c.73	3 parts / SSbc / second half 18th century	pp. 1-3, 25-27, 47-49	**316**
266	Ms. Mus. c.95	S / late 17th century–early 18th century	pp. 72-73 p. 95 p. 132 p. 124 p. 70	**300.B.7 (378)** **342** **349** **350** **353**
267	Ms. Mus. d.8	S / bc / *ca.*1750	fols. 71-72	**341**
268	Ms. Mus. d.149	S / 18th century	pp. 27-30 pp. 64-65	**102** **105**
269	Ms. Mus. d.152	S / *ca.*1740–second half 18th century	pp. 135-136	**102**
270	Ms. Mus. d.155	A / 18th century	pp. 6-9	**110**
271	Ms. Mus. d.156	A / 18th century	pp. 182-189 pp. 268, 270	**105** **110**
272	Ms. Mus. d.157	A / fourth quarter 18th century	pp. 17-21	**117**
273	Ms. Mus. d.158	A / 18th century	pp. 180-183	**110**
274	Ms. Mus. d.159	A / fourth quarter 18th century	fols. 20v-21	**117**
275	Ms. Mus. d.160	T / 18th century	pp. 220-223	**110**
276	Ms. Mus. d.163	B / 18th century	fols. 86v-88	**110**
277	Ms. Mus. d.165	B / 18th century	p. 221 pp. 215-218 pp. 143-148	**102** **105** **110**
278	Ms. Mus. e.18	score / *ca.*1790 / book of hymns / voice parts vary	fols. 89v-90 fols. 25v-26 fol. 22 fol. 118v fol. 15 fol. 24v fol. 14v	**520** **522** **523** **524** **527** **529** **530**
279	Ms. Mus. Sch. E.397	keyboard score / first half 18th century	p. 45 pp. 32-33 pp. 48-49	**436** **438** **453**
280	Ms. Mus. Sch. G.615	violin / first quarter 18th century	p. 41 p. 12	**336** **436**

Och: Christ Church, Oxford

281	Mus. 3	score / first half 18th century	fols. 41-44	**310**
282	Mus. 46	keyboard score / first quarter 18th century	fol. 59v fol. 60	**437** **452**
283	Mus. 48	score / first quarter 18th century	pp. 100-121 pp. 86-100	**106** **119**
284	Mus. 363	keyboard score / first quarter 18th century	fols. 5v-6	**403.2**
285	Mus. 620	score / first quarter 18th century	fol. 11	**310.5**

GREAT BRITAIN

INDEX OF PRINTED COLLECTIONS

Guide

This index is limited to those collections from before 1800 which contain works by Clarke. Works printed and sold as single sheet folios are not included in this index. These sources are cited with library reference numbers in the main body of the catalog.

In the case of congregational Psalms and hymns which appear in modern hymnals, the name of the hymnal is given within the main body of the catalog. This is not intended to be an exhaustive list of all modern hymnals containing hymns using melodies by Clarke. The references are made to enable the reader to locate the hymn in an easily accessible modern printing.

This Index of Printed Collections is arranged alphabetically by title. To facilitate cross reference between this list and the entry for each composition, a number is assigned to each, the first three letters of the first key word and a digit. One library copy seen by the author is cited for each to facilitate location. For the location of other copies see the *International Inventory of Musical Sources* (RISM).

Each entry contains:

    1. Printed collection number.
    2. Title, editor, publisher and date of publication.
    3. Library catalog number of one selected copy.
    4. Foliation, numeration, or pagination in the source given, when available.
    5. Entry number of the works by Clarke in the Thematic Catalog.

ABR 1	An Abridgement of the new version of the psalms, . . . Edited with preface by Thomas Johnson. London: 1777.	Lbm: A.511.d	fol. 9	**169**
ALA 1	The Alamode musician being a new collection of songs compos'd by some of the most eminent masters, . . . London: H. Playford, 1698.	Lbm: G.91	fols. 6v-7	**352**
ANC 1	Ancient psalmody from the publications of Thomas Est, . . . London: Chappell, n.d.	Lbm: E.414	p. 20 p. 39	**169** **170**
APO 1	Apollo's banquet newly revived: containing new and easie instructions for the treble-violin . . . London: W. Pearson for H. Playford, 1701.	DRc: Mus. C.75	no. 21 no. 47 no. 92	**437** **453** **482**

APO 1	Apollo's banquet newly revived . . . [*continued*]	DRc: Mus. C.75	no. 12	**483**
			no. 11	**486**
			no. 40	**488**
			no. 13	**489**
			no. 134	**490**
			no. 38	**493**
			no. 10	**494**
BLA 1	Bland's collection of divine music, consisting of psalms, hymns and anthems . . . London: J. Bland, (1790).	Lbm: H.817	p. 88	**171**
BOO 1	A Book of Psalmody. Containing a choice Collection of Psalm-Tunes, Hymns and Anthems, . . . Collected, printed, taught and sold by M. Wilkins . . . London: *ca.*1730. London: *ca.*1750, another edition called A Second Book of Psalmody.	Lbm: A.992	p. 49	**114**
BOO 2	A Book of Psalmody containing Chanting-Tunes . . . (continuation of title differs with edition). Edited by James Green. London: 1734-1751.			
	9th ed.	Lbm: C.73.a		
	11th ed.	Lbm: C.73		
	8th-11th eds.			**114**
BOO 3	A Book of Psalmody, containing Variety of Tunes for all the Common Metres of the Psalms . . . And Fifteen Anthems, all set in Four Parts, etc. Edited by John Chetham, Wm. Pearson for Joseph Turner.			
	1st ed.: Sheffield, 1718	Lbm: B.611.f	p. 77	**114**
	3rd ed.: Halifax, 1724	Lbm: B.611	p. 30	**114**
BOO 4	A Book of Psalm-Tunes, by W. Langhorne. 2nd ed. London: 1723.		p. 67	**114**
BRO 1	Michael Broom's Collection of Church Music. Isleworrh: *ca.*1725.		p. 43	**114**
BRO 2	Michael Broom's collection of church music for the use of his scholars. Birmingham: M. Broome, *ca.*1750-1765.	Bp: 427002	fols. 61-64	**113**
CAT 1	The Second Book of the Catch club or merry companions being a choice collection of the most diverting catches . . . London: Walsh, (1732).	Ckc: 112.77.Res	p. 35	**390**
			p. 45	**391**
CAT 2	The Catch club, or pleasant musical companion . . . Birmingham: M. Broome, *ca.*1740.	Lbm: G.88	p. 3	**391**
			p. 2	**550**
CAT 3	———. *Idem,* 1757.	Lbm: G.88	p. 3	**391**
			p. 2	**550**

SAC 1	Sacred harmony . . . selected from the works of . . . Clark, etc . . . Arranged by R. Willoughby. London: printed for the editor, 1795?	Lbm: A.1095	pp. 111-116	**105**
SAC 2	Sacred melody, being a choice collection of anthems. Edited by Abraham Milner. London: (1750).	Lbm: A.1039	pp. 13-14	**108**
			p. 17	**114**
SAC 3	Sacred mirth: or the pious soul's daily delight, being a choice . . . collection of psalms, hymns, anthems, and canons on various divine subjects. Edited by W. Tans'ur. London: A. Pearson and Hodges, 1739.	Lbm: C.101	p. 34	**172**
SAC 4	Sacred music for one, . . . and four voices . . . ; 3 vols. Adapted and arranged by R. J. Stevens. London: printed for the editor, (*ca.* 1798-1802).	Lbm: H.819		
	Vol. 2		pp. 96-99	**102**
	A Second Book of Psalmody . . . See BOO 1			
SEL 1	Select lessons for the violin as preludes almands sarabands corants minuets and jiggs as also the newest country dances now in use fairly engraven. London: J. Walsh and J. Hare, 1702.	DRc: Mus. C.77	fol. 10	**353**
			fol. 13	**432**
			fol. 12	**467**
SEL 2	Select portions of the psalms of David for the use of parish-churches . . . 2nd ed. London: H. Gardner, 1786.	Lbm: A.1230.KK	item 2	**165**
			item 35	**169**
			item 5	**171**
SEL 3	Select psalms of David, in the old version . . . Stamford: W. Harrod, 1789.	Lbm: C.732.a	item 3	**165**
SEL 4	The first, second and third books of the Self-instructor on the violin: or the art of playing on that instrument, improv'd & made easy . . . London: printed for and sold by J. Hare, 1700.	DRc: Mus.C.76 & 77		
	Vol. 2		fol. 14	**337**
	Vol. 2		fol. 21	**338**
	Vol. 2		fol. 20	**363**
	Vol. 3		fol. 17	**435**
	Vol. 2		fol. 2	**488**
	Vol. 2		fol. 2	**493**
SET 1	A Sett of New Psalm-Tunes and Anthems. Edited by William Knapp. 2nd to 8th editions. London: 1741-1770. (No. **110**, attributed to "a very eminent master")			**110**
SIX 1	Six select anthems in score . . . for two or three voices . . . by Dr. Croft, Dr. Blow, H. Purcell, and J. Clarke. London: printed for W. Randall, 1770.	Lbm: G.517.n.(1.)	p. 20	**105**
			pp. 28-36	**119**
SOC 1	Social harmony. Consisting of a collection of songs and catches . . . Edited by T. Hale. 4 vols. in 8. London: 1763. (No. **391**, Pt. 3)	Lbm: D.383	p. 19	**391**

WIT 1	With and mirth; or, pills to purge melancholy . . . many of the songs being new set. London: W. Pearson for H. Playford, 1699.	Lcm: C.117.a.119	p. 244	**336**
			p. 246	**338**
			p. 327	**342**
			p. 251	**349**
			pp. 296-297	**350**
			pp. 247-248	**363**
			p. 245	**370**
			pp. 233-234	**541**
WIT 2	——— . 2nd ed., corrected, with additions, 1705.			**363**
				342
WIT 3	——— . 2nd ed. Vol. 4. Corrected by J. Lenton, 1706.	Lbm: 1346.a.31	p. 45	**301.B.3 (339)**
			pp. 298-299	**347**
			p. 65	**368**
			pp. 57-58	**380**
			pp. 290-291	**384**
WIT 4	——— . 3rd ed. Vol. 1. Printed by W. Pearson, 1707.	Lbm: 1346.a.28	p. 244	**336**
			p. 246	**338**
			p. 327	**342**
			pp. 128-129	**346**
			p. 251	**349**
			pp. 296-297	**350**
			p. 120	**354**
			p. 247	**363**
			p. 245	**370**
			p. 233	**541**
WIT 5	——— . 3rd ed. Vol. 1. London: printed by W. Pearson for J. Cullen, 1707.		p. 327	**342**
			pp. 233-234	**363**
WIT 6	——— . 2nd ed. Vol. 3. Printed by W. Pearson, 1707.	Lbm: 1346a.30	pp. 53-54	**353**
			pp. 176-177	**367**
WIT 7	——— . Vol. 4. London: printed by W. Pearson for J. Young, corrected by J. Lenton, 1707.		p. 45	**301.B.3 (339)**
			p. 298	**347**
			p. 65	**368**
			pp. 57-58	**380**
			pp. 290-291	**384**
WIT 8	——— . 2nd ed. Vol. 4. London: printed by W. Pearson for J. Young, corrected by J. Lenton, 1709.	Lbm: 238.g.43	p. 45	**301.B.3 (339)**
			pp. 158-159	**343**
			pp. 298-299	**347**
			pp. 140-141	**300.C (355)**
			p. 65	**368**
			pp. 57-58	**380**
			pp. 284-286	**383**
			pp. 290-291	**384**
WIT 9	——— . 3rd ed., with enlarged additions. Vol. 3. London: printed by W. Pearson, 1712.	Lbm: 238.g.42	pp. 53-54	**353**
			p. 194	**359**
			pp. 176-177	**367**
			pp. 205-206	**371**